HOMEBOUND

Falkirk Council Library Services

This book is due for return on or before the l   dicated on the
label. Renewals may be obtained o   ion.

MR MONK IS A MESS

MR MONK IS A MESS

Lee Goldberg

CHIVERS

British Library Cataloguing in Publication Data available

This Large Print edition published by AudioGO Ltd, Bath, 2013.
Published by arrangement with NAL SIGNET, a division of Penguin Group (USA) Inc.

U.K. Hardcover   ISBN 978 1 4713 2546 5
U.K. Softcover   ISBN 978 1 4713 2547 2

Printed and bound in Great Britain by
MPG Books Group Limited

To Valerie and Maddie

AUTHOR'S NOTE AND ACKNOWLEDGMENTS

This book is one of the few in the series that was written entirely at my desk in Los Angeles, California. I did all of my traveling this time courtesy of Google Earth.

The story takes place immediately after the events in *Mr. Monk on Patrol* — but don't worry, you won't be missing anything if you haven't read that one yet (though it will be more satisfying if you do). It also continues a narrative arc in Monk and Natalie's relationship that began, more or less, in *Mr. Monk and the Dirty Cop* and has evolved over the past five Monk mysteries.

The early part of this book takes place in Summit, New Jersey. There is a real town of that name that bears some striking similarities to the one in this story, but mine is entirely fictional in its geography, history, and political structure.

I want to thank William Rabkin, Terence Winter, Frank Cardea, and George Schenk for their invaluable help with this story, and Andy Breckman, the creator of *Monk,* for giving me so much creative freedom with these books and with his characters. But this novel would not have been written at all if not for the continued support of Gina Maccoby and Kerry Donovan.

Finally, this is the first time I've written a *Monk* book without having to call upon Dr. D. P. Lyle for his wise medical or forensic advice, but I am thanking him anyway because I knew I could call him, day or night, if a question *did* come up.

I hope you enjoy the book and, if you do, that you'll drop by www.leegoldberg.com or give me a tweet @leegoldberg and let me know.

CHAPTER ONE:
MR. MONK IN SUMMIT

The hours pass very slowly when you're sitting in a squad car, parked behind a billboard on a New Jersey country road, waiting for speeders to whiz by.

It's not the most glamorous side of law enforcement, but writing $390 speeding tickets pays the bills, especially when a handful of corrupt politicians have looted the town treasury to finance their outrageously extravagant lifestyles.

So that's why Adrian Monk and I — the lovely and resourceful Natalie Teeger — had to do our stint early that Monday morning out on the old highway, a remote, curving stretch of two-lane asphalt through the rolling hills, which no driver could resist taking at high speed.

We were into our third week working as uniformed police officers in Summit, thousands of miles away from our homes in San Francisco, where Monk was usually em-

9

ployed as a police consultant and I toiled, underpaid and underappreciated, as his long-suffering assistant.

Summit was basically an upscale bedroom community for highly educated, well-off professionals who worked in New York City, which was only a thirty-minute train ride away. The town's roots as a pastoral farming community were still evident in the pastoral setting, the tree-lined streets, and the lush landscaping around the homes, many of which dated back to the early 1900s and had been impeccably restored and maintained. That cost lots of money, but from what I could see, there was no shortage of that in Summit, except in the recently looted town treasury.

We were in Summit as a favor to Police Chief Randy Disher, who'd once been a San Francisco homicide detective, and his live-in girlfriend, Sharona Fleming, who'd once been Monk's nurse and assistant.

With all the local politicians in jail or out on bail awaiting trial, Disher found himself drafted as acting mayor and in desperate need of temporary help enforcing the law. So he called on us.

I'd worked around a lot of cops over the years while helping Monk solve murders but I'd never had a badge myself. But now that

10

I'd worn one for a few weeks, I'd discovered that I liked it.

"Thank God for cars and paved roads," Monk said. He sat in the passenger seat, aiming his radar gun out the window, waiting for our next victim.

I had to think about the reasoning behind his comment because Monk reasoned like nobody else. That's partly a result of his obsessive-compulsive disorder, but mostly it's due to the bizarre way he looks at the world. It's what makes him a brilliant detective and an enormous pain in the ass.

I knew he liked cars because they had four wheels and were symmetrical, but he also firmly believed that the steering wheel should be in the center of the dashboard instead of on one side or the other. He would have settled for cars having two steering wheels, one on each side, even if one was only for show, but so far none of the major automakers had agreed to his gracious compromise (despite the fact that he'd sent them countless letters arguing his point).

So why was he thanking God for cars now? Perhaps it had less to do with cars than with the pavement, which I knew he liked without reservation.

"You're grateful because cars are symmetrical," I said, "and the roads they use are flat, level, and divided into lanes that dictate an orderly flow of traffic."

"That's only part of it," he said. "I'm eternally grateful that nobody has to use horses for transportation anymore. Back in the old days, before we had paved roads, horses should have been outlawed in populated areas."

"That would have made it awfully difficult for people to get around."

"Horses made it worse."

"I don't see how."

"On a typical day in New York City in the 1800s, horses dropped two-point-five million pounds of manure and expelled sixty-five thousand gallons of urine onto dirt roads. You try walking through that." Monk did a full-body shudder, which people unfamiliar with him often mistook for an epileptic seizure instead of extreme revulsion. "Before cars came along, the Big Apple was the Big Poop."

Ever since Monk had become improbably enamored of Ellen Morse, the ecologically conscious and obsessive-compulsive proprietor of Poop, a store on Summit's main street that sold an astonishing array of art, shampoos, creams, stationery, fossils, coffee, and cooking oils derived from excrement, he'd been a walking encyclopedia of crap.

"I never thought of it from that perspective," I said. "And I'm sorry that I can now."

"It's a wonder humanity survived that apocalypse."

"That wasn't an apocalypse," I said.

"When the streets are piled with four hundred thousand tons of poo soaked in twenty-three million, seven hundred and twenty-five thousand gallons of pee in a year, that's an apocalypse," Monk said. "That's why four horsemen, and not four guys in Toyotas, are your first warning that it's coming."

I sighed and shook my head. I couldn't believe we were having this stupid discussion when there were far more important things we could be talking about, like the enormous changes we were making in our lives.

In forty-eight hours we'd be back in San Francisco, but only for a few weeks, and just to pack up our lives and our belongings. That's because Disher had offered us full-time jobs as cops on his force and we'd accepted.

Well, I had.

Monk kept flip-flopping.

But no matter what he ultimately decided,

our relationship had already changed in a big way. From the moment I put on the Summit Police uniform, I stopped being his employee and became his partner, although I couldn't bring myself to call him by his first name.

And if he decided to stay in San Francisco, and I came back to Summit, he'd have to decide whether to hire a new assistant or to try to make it on his own for the first time since his wife was killed and he was discharged from the SFPD on psychological grounds.

I was about to bring up the topic when a bright red, mud-splattered Range Rover sped past the billboard we were hiding behind and on toward Summit.

Monk lowered his radar gun and looked at me. "Let's roll."

I flicked on the lights, cranked up the siren, and punched the gas, peeling out in a spray of gravel. The driver of the Range Rover wasn't the only one who couldn't resist speeding on that lonely highway.

We caught up to the Range Rover in seconds and the driver dutifully pulled over to the shoulder without a fight.

I parked a few feet behind the car and observed that the driver was a woman and that the vehicle had New Jersey plates.

14

Monk was scowling, presumably because her bumper was splashed with mud thick with twigs and bits of leaves. He hated dirt.

I typed the numbers into the computer on our center console and discovered the Range Rover was registered to Kelsey Turek of Summit. There were no wants or warrants associated with her or the vehicle.

I got out and approached the driver's side of the car and the woman at the wheel. Monk remained behind me, on the passenger side of the car, peering into the back of the vehicle, just in case there were a couple of bank robbers, a kidnapped heiress, a dozen illegal aliens, piles of cocaine, or maybe a stolen nuclear warhead in plain sight. The backseat was folded down flat, but the cargo area was empty. All I saw was a bottle of vinegar on the floor. As far as I knew, that wasn't contraband.

The woman lowered her window as I approached. The first thing I noticed was the heavenly smell of the Range Rover's plush leather interior. I'd never owned a car upholstered in anything but vinyl or cloth.

The driver was a cute, pug-nosed woman in her thirties, wearing a man's long-sleeve flannel shirt and a pair of faded jeans. Her face was red around her eyes and the bridge

15

of her nose, as if she'd been wearing ski goggles.

"Good morning," I said. "May I see your license and registration, please?"

She already had them out on her lap and handed them to me. She had a nasty blister on her palm, just below her thumb.

"What's the problem, Officer?" she asked.

I glanced at her license, which identified her as Kelsey Turek, though her photo reminded me of Katie Holmes in her *Dawson's Creek* days, before *Batman*, Tom Cruise, Scientology, and age robbed her of that adorable woman-child quality.

"Are you aware of the speed limit on this highway?" I asked.

"Fifty-five," she said.

"And do you know how fast you were driving, Ms. Turek?"

"Fifty-five," she said.

"Perhaps it would surprise you to know the actual speed you were driving," I said and realized I didn't know, either. I looked across the top of the car to Monk, who stood on the passenger side and was peering through the window at Turek. "How fast was she going, Mr. Monk?"

"Fifty-four," he said.

I glared at him. "So why did we pull her over? Was it so you could commend her for

16

traveling at an even-numbered rate of speed or ticket her for driving too slow and impeding the nonexistent traffic?"

"Her car is splattered with mud," Monk said. "And there's a piece of a plastic bag caught on her trailer hitch."

"That's not a traffic violation," I said.

"May I go now?" Turek asked, looking uncomfortable, like a child watching her parents arguing.

I handed her back her driver's license and registration. I saw a white band of skin at the base of the ring finger on her left hand where she'd perhaps taken off a wedding ring. It made me think of the one that I'd once worn.

It was years after Mitch was shot down over Kosovo before I finally stopped wearing my ring. It took a surprisingly long time for that band of pale skin to tan and I was painfully sad when it did.

"Officer?" she prodded.

"Yes, I'm sorry," I said. "You can go."

"No, you can't," Monk said to her.

I sighed and turned back to Turek. "Forgive me for asking, but would you mind washing your car when you get back to Summit? My partner would really appreciate it."

"Sure thing," she said. "Whatever you

17

want, Officer."

"We can't let her go and we certainly can't let her wash her car," Monk said.

"Why not?" I demanded.

"Because she could wash away important evidence."

"Of *what?*" I said. "That her car was dirty?"

"That she murdered her husband," Monk said.

That last word was barely out of his mouth when Turek floored it, the car speeding away, spraying us with loose dirt and gravel.

I staggered back, my face stung by the bits of rock, my eyes full of dirt.

"I'll take that as a confession," Monk said.

CHAPTER TWO:
MR. MONK GIVES CHASE

"What the hell?" I said, still stunned by Kelsey Turek's unexpected and very sudden flight.

"Don't just stand there in a daze," Monk said. "She's getting away."

I hurried back to the car, blinking hard as I ran, trying to clear my eyes. We got in, I hit the siren, and we raced after Turek's Range Rover. I still had a speck of something in one eye and kept blinking until I had tears rolling down my cheeks.

Monk took the radio and called the dispatcher, informing her that we were now in pursuit of a killer. He didn't even qualify his statement by saying "suspected" killer because he was that sure of himself. And he had every right to be. He was never wrong when it came to homicide — but that didn't make his unexpected pronouncements of guilt or smug self-confidence any less irritating.

We closed in on the Range Rover, which was going about ninety miles an hour now, and one of my tears finally washed the speck from my eye.

"We can add driving at excessive speed to her list of heinous crimes," Monk said, then looked at me. "Don't worry, Natalie, it's okay. We'll catch her."

"I'm not crying," I said, wiping the tears away with the back of my hand. "Why would I be crying?"

Monk shrugged. "Shame? Embarrassment? A crippling sense of inadequacy?"

There was a truck ahead of Kelsey. She swerved around it, right into oncoming traffic. Two cars veered off the road onto the shoulder to avoid her. One of the cars crashed through a fence into an open field, the other spun out.

I had to slow down to weave around the truck and the two cars while Kelsey gained even more distance, disappearing around a curve.

"What the hell are you talking about?" I asked Monk.

"I'm answering your question," he said.

"I had something in my eye, that's all," I said. "But what I'd like to know is why you think I'd feel inadequate."

"Because you're crying over almost letting

20

a murderer go."

"I had no idea she was a murderer," I said.

"That's what I mean," he said. "Are you going to start crying again now?"

"No, because I don't have anything in my eye anymore," I said as we caught up to Kelsey's Range Rover. "What makes you think that she murdered her husband? Was there a corpse in the back of her car that I didn't see?"

"Of course not. She has already disposed of the body. She covered the body with black plastic garbage bags, dragged it out of the car into a shallow grave, poured lye over it, and then buried it."

Turek's Range Rover charged up behind a Honda Accord and passed it, intentionally sideswiping the vehicle as she went by.

The driver of the Accord, startled and fighting for control of his car, swerved wildly across both lanes, cutting us off and forcing us onto the inclined shoulder to avoid a collision.

Our car tipped hard to the right, slamming Monk against the door as I raced along the shoulder. We passed the Accord and then I wrenched the wheel hard to the left, vaulting our car back up onto the asphalt with a sharp bounce, setting off sparks that I could see reflected in the side-view mirror.

Turek had managed to gain even more ground on us. I floored the gas pedal and tightened my grip on the wheel.

"How can you possibly know that's what happened?" I asked.

"Because I am not legally blind," he said.

"You really don't want to criticize me while I'm in the middle of a high-speed pursuit, Mr. Monk. Just give me the facts, okay, so I know why the hell I'm doing this."

"The organic matter in the mud on her car clearly indicates that she was in the forest. You can see where some of the mud was dragged off her rear bumper when she pulled out something heavy wrapped in a black plastic trash bag from the cargo area," Monk said. "The bag snagged on her trailer hitch, leaving a shred of plastic behind."

"That doesn't mean she killed her husband and dumped his corpse."

We were now only a few yards behind her vehicle and closing fast.

"The missing wedding ring indicates there was tension in her marriage and the fresh, disgusting blister on her palm is clearly from digging with a shovel."

"It is?"

"She should have been wearing leather work gloves," Monk said. "Instead, she was wearing rubber gloves, which protected her hands from the lye, but not from the friction of holding the shovel handle while digging. For further protection, she was also wearing a long-sleeve shirt, jeans, and goggles, which she cinched too tight, hence the redness on her face. After she buried the body, she got rid of the shovel, her goggles and gloves, and the lye somewhere, but she forgot about the unopened jug of vinegar, perhaps because in and of itself it wasn't obviously incriminating."

"What's the vinegar for?" I looked ahead to see if there was any traffic apart from the SUV we were pursuing. There wasn't.

"To neutralize any lye that got on her skin before it burned her."

"Vinegar neutralizes lye?"

"You didn't know that?"

"Why would I know that?" I asked.

"Basic human survival. It's like asking if I know how much exposure to radiation is fatal or how long I'll live from a rattlesnake bite without medical attention."

"I don't know either of those things."

"It's a wonder you're alive."

Now I really did want to cry, and not because his brilliant deduction made me feel stupid for missing everything. It was because *I didn't miss any of it.*

For the first time, after years of training myself to be more observant, I'd finally managed to see all the details that he did. I saw the mud and the scrap of the Hefty bag on her trailer hitch. I noticed how she was dressed, the blister on her hand, her missing wedding ring, and the impression the tight goggles had left on her face. I even saw the bottle of vinegar.

And I *still* couldn't put all the pieces together.

How dense could I possibly be?

Maybe it was because I lacked his extreme sense of order.

Maybe it was because I didn't have all the obscure knowledge that he did.

Or maybe it was because I just didn't have his gift.

No matter how hard I tried, I doubted I'd ever be as observant as he was or have the insight, the *artistry,* to recognize the significance of what I saw.

On the other hand, there was the very real possibility that his talent for detecting arose from his crippling psychological disorder, one that had deprived him of enjoying so many of the simple and profound pleasures in life that I'd experienced.

It wasn't a trade I would like to make.

Perhaps, I thought, it was time that I accepted my limitations.

The hell I will.

I pressed the gas pedal harder and edged past Turek on her driver's side until the patrol car's right-front edge was near the left side of her rear bumper.

"Careful," Monk said. "You're going to hit her."

"That's the idea," I said.

"Are you insane?"

That's when I executed a standard Pursuit Intervention Technique maneuver, something I'd seen cops do on the news in real-life car chases but that I'd never tried myself, mainly because I'd never had a reason to before.

I turned to the right and clipped the edge of the SUV. The Range Rover abruptly spun sideways directly in front of us and I rammed it, pushing it off the road onto the shoulder, Monk shrieking in terror the whole way, his hands pressed against the dash.

I stopped the car, quite pleased with myself. I hadn't solved the murder but at least I was able to pull off the PIT maneuver without any training besides sitting in front of the evening news.

Monk and I both got out, our guns drawn and aimed at the vehicle. The air bags in

25

Turek's car had deployed and one had burst open right in her face. She was sitting in the driver's seat, unhurt but dazed, as we approached her vehicle.

"Come out with your hands up," I said.

Turek blinked hard and looked at me as if waking from a dream.

"Now," I said. "Nice and slow."

She opened the door and staggered out, immediately collapsing to her knees on the pavement, more out of dizziness than submission.

While Monk kept her covered with his gun, I holstered my weapon, got behind her, and cuffed her hands behind her back.

"You're under arrest for murder," I said.

"I don't believe this," she said. "How did you know what I did?"

I looked up at Monk, who holstered his weapon, rolled his shoulders, and tipped his head from side to side, setting himself and the world right again.

"We're police officers," Monk said.

CHAPTER THREE:
MR. MONK AND
THE TALKING CAR

Randy Disher, Summit police chief and acting mayor, showed up in his Suburban police cruiser twenty minutes after the forensics team, the tow trucks, and the paramedics, who I'd called for Turek just to be on the safe side. He was in full uniform, and that included a wide-brimmed Ranger-style hat with the Summit police emblem on the front, which appeared too big not only for his head but for his body as well.

Despite the powerful leadership positions he now held, Disher still looked like an eager-to-please boy to me and I had a hard time taking him as seriously as he wanted to be taken, especially since we'd been friends for so long. But I made the effort because I genuinely liked him and he was, after all, my present employer.

He surveyed the wrecked cars, which the forensics team was examining and photographing, and glanced at Turek — who sat handcuffed in the back of an ambulance, being checked out by the paramedics — before he finally worked his way over to where we were standing, on the side of the road.

"You caught a murderer before anyone knew a murder had been committed," Disher said. "That's impressive even for you, Monk."

"Thank you, Chief," Monk said.

"I wish you could have apprehended her without smashing a quarter of our fleet in the process."

"That's her fault," Monk said, pointing at me.

"Thanks for the support, partner," I said.

"I also wish you had evidence," Disher said. "You know, something like a dead body, before you decided to run her off the road."

"She fled the instant Mr. Monk accused her of killing her husband," I said.

"Freaking out isn't quite the same thing as a confession," Disher said.

"She also asked how we knew what she did," I said, "which is sort of like a confession."

"It's not," Disher said, "but even if it was, did she ask you the question before or after you read Mrs. Turek her rights?"

"Before," I said glumly.

"Has she told you where she buried the body?"

I shook my head. "She's not talking and has demanded a lawyer."

Disher sighed. "So, in other words, we have nothing but a smashed hundred-thousand-dollar Range Rover, a smashed police car, and Monk's hunch."

"There's more," Monk said.

"I certainly hope so," Disher said.

Monk told him about the blister, the missing wedding ring, the bottle of vinegar, the shred of plastic bag, and the leafy mud on her bumper.

"Which means," Disher said, "that all we have to hold her on is a speeding ticket and reckless driving."

I cleared my throat. "We didn't give her a ticket."

"Because she sped off before you could write it?" Disher asked.

"Because she wasn't speeding," I replied. "That wasn't why we pulled her over."

Disher looked at Monk. "Are you telling me that all she had to do was drive by and you knew that she was a murderer?"

"No," Monk said. "Of course not."

"Then why did you stop her?"

"Her car was filthy," Monk said.

"So you pulled her over without any probable cause whatsoever and then you accused her of being a murderer."

"She is," Monk said.

"No wonder she sped off. She thought you were insane." Disher took off his hat, regarded it for a moment as he held it by the rim, then threw it like a Frisbee out into the open field beside the highway. The three of us watched the hat sail through the air, then land in the tall weeds.

"What did you do that for?" Monk asked.

"Because I'm finished," Disher said, tipping his head toward Kelsey Turek. "She's a very rich woman. She's going to sue us and when she wins, and owns Summit outright, the first thing she's going to do, even before she renames the place Kelseyville, is throw me out."

"Would it help if we found the body?" Monk said.

"Yes, Monk, that would make a big difference."

"She may not want to talk," Monk said. "But her car will."

He marched over to her Range Rover and we trailed after him. I thought I knew what he had in mind and I wanted to stop him before he made a big mistake.

"We can't look at her GPS navigation

system without a warrant, Mr. Monk, because if we do, and we find the body as a result, the evidence will be thrown out as fruit from the poisonous tree and she'll walk."

Disher gave me a look. "You watch a lot of *Law & Order,* don't you?"

"What do you think I do in San Francisco when we don't have a case to investigate and I'm stuck in Mr. Monk's apartment while he cleans?"

"Contemplate suicide?"

"Now you know why I accepted your job offer," I said.

"I don't need to access her GPS unit to know where this car has been," Monk said.

He walked around the vehicle, his hands stretched out in front of him, framing his point of view. He stopped here and there to crouch, cock his head, stand on his tiptoes, and basically examine the car from every angle. When he was done, he turned to us and presented his findings.

"There are pine needles, bark, and decaying leaves in the mud, which indicates she was in a forested area," he said.

"That's a big help," Disher said.

"Thank you," Monk said, oblivious to Disher's sarcasm. "But there's more. The dirt on the car was still moist when we stopped her, so, given the composition of the mud, the amount of water in it, the temperature and humidity of the environment, and the speed at which she was driving, I believe she couldn't have traveled more than five miles from the grave."

"You know how fast mud dries?" Disher said.

"Of course I do," Monk said. "It's a matter of basic human survival."

"It is?" Disher asked.

I spoke up. "It's like knowing what a fatal dose of radiation is or how long you'll live after a rattlesnake bites you."

"I've never been exposed to deadly levels of radiation," Disher said, "or been bitten by a rattlesnake."

"Yet," Monk said.

"Let's say you're right about how fast mud dries," Disher said. "Knowing the body is within a five-mile radius doesn't narrow it down much."

"It will when we find the skunk," Monk said.

"What skunk?" I asked.

"The dead one that she ran over." Monk pointed to the wheels. "There's fur and bits of flesh stuck in the front and rear passenger-side wheel wells."

"Gee, she really was on a killing spree

today," I said. "No living thing in her path was safe."

"Actually, the skunk was already dead when she drove over it," Monk said, "or there would be much more blood."

"How do you know it was a skunk?" I asked.

"I can smell it," Monk said. "Can't you?"

"No," I said.

"The odor is overpowering," he said. "It's almost as strong as the egg-and-cheese burrito the chief had for breakfast."

"You can smell that on me?" Disher said.

"I can also see it," Monk said. "You dribbled some on your shirt."

Disher examined his shirt, finding the tiny spot on his stomach. "Damn. How do you know she drove over the road-kill after she left the grave and not before she arrived there?"

"The skunk matter is stuck on the mud rather than coated with it," he said. "If we find the dead skunk, we'll know we are in the right vicinity."

"And then what?" Disher said. "How will you know where to go from there?"

Monk crouched by the right side of the Range Rover's front bumper. "It appears that she was going too fast when she turned onto a narrow, rust-colored mud road, and she clipped a post or a tree, shattering her fog light." Monk pointed to the scratched bumper and the broken light below it. "There is mud inside the fog light casing, which means it was broken before she went on the dirt road. All you have to do is go back five miles, look for a dead skunk, an unpaved road with rust-colored mud, and an object with scrapes of red automotive paint on it. You'll know you're in the right spot when you see the broken glass and the unique tire impressions from this vehicle in the mud."

"Well, if that's all there is to it, why are you still standing here? Call me when you find the grave."

And with that, Disher went out to retrieve his hat and we drove off to find where Kelsey Turek had buried her husband.

Twenty minutes later, we found the shallow grave and secured the scene. And ten minutes after that, we found the bottle of lye, the shovel, the gloves, and the goggles in a gas station Dumpster a mile from the dirt road.

Once we found her husband's body, Kelsey Turek decided to ignore her right to remain silent and instead energetically exercised her right to get everything off her surgically enhanced chest.

Disher drove us all back into Summit in his Suburban. On the way, Turek told us her tragic tale, which she prefaced by telling us all about the rich and wonderful life that she, a literary agent, and her husband, Rick, a Manhattan architect, had enjoyed during their ten years of marriage.

They had a beautiful home in Summit, a beach house in Maine, and four European cars. They were connoisseurs of exquisite wine, collectors of fine art, and masters of tantric sex.

"We could go for hours," she said. "Sometimes even days."

"Stopping only to open a bottle of wine and admire one of your paintings," I said.

"I am only trying to give you some background so you will appreciate my actions from the proper perspective," she said.

"Let her talk," Disher told me.

Yesterday at breakfast, Rick calmly informed her that they were penniless, a consequence of his long, secret addiction to online gambling.

But the news was even worse. When he'd used up all of their money, emptying their accounts, maxing out their credit cards, and leveraging their property, he'd embezzled three hundred thousand dollars from his firm, which he also lost. The firm just discovered the missing money, so she'd realized that he'd most likely be going to jail very soon, leaving her to deal with their financial mess.

Kelsey got up from the table without saying a word, found the heaviest frying pan they owned, and hit him on the head with it a few times.

She dragged his body to the garage, put Hefty trash bags over him, sealed them tight with duct tape, and then put his body into the Range Rover.

Kelsey was thankful that she was strong enough to do all of this without having to cut his body into pieces.

"All of those hours of Pilates and tantric sex really paid off," she said. "I've got the body fat of a gazelle."

After that, she spent an hour on the Internet doing research on the best ways to dispose of a body and settled on burying him and covering him with lye to speed decomposition. All she had to figure out was where she should bury the corpse.

She recalled a piece of land that her husband had considered buying as investment property a few years back, right before the real estate bubble burst. It was nearby, but forested enough to offer seclusion and the strong possibility that his body wouldn't be found before it turned to mush.

So she bought the supplies and then, in the wee hours of the morning, drove out to the plot of land and buried him. It took her all night, but she got the job done. She ditched the shovel, lye, gloves, and goggles on the way home.

"I bet that everyone would think that he fled to avoid arrest and it wouldn't occur to anyone that his poor shocked and devastated wife had killed him," she said. "But apparently I'm as luckless a gambler as Rick was."

I couldn't argue with her on that point, nor could I particularly blame her for what she did. In fact, I thought she had a pretty good chance at getting sympathy from a jury, but I kept that opinion to myself.

Her lawyer was waiting for her when we got back to police headquarters. Disher told us he was one of the most expensive and respected criminal attorneys in the state. But when the attorney learned that she'd spilled her guts to us, he abruptly quit as her counsel. I think his resignation had less to do with her confession than his realization that she was broke. Disher got her a public defender.

While all of this was going on, we wrote up our reports and then submitted them to

Disher in his office.

"It was a stroke of brilliance inviting you two out here," Disher said. "It's that kind of bold, decisive action that got me where I am today."

"I thought it was Sharona's idea to bring Mr. Monk here to help out," I said.

"Yes, but I didn't hesitate to act on it," Disher said.

"And to take the credit for it," I said.

Disher got up, looked around the empty squad room, then closed the door and turned back to me. "Natalie, I'm the chief of police here, remember? You need to be much more intimidated by me, at least around the office."

"Sorry, Randy. I'll work on it," I said.

He groaned. " 'Randy'?"

"Sorry, Chief," I said. "It's hard for me. I guess I've known you too long as good old Randy, Captain Stottlemeyer's right-hand man."

"And I've always known you as Monk's assistant, driving him around and handing him wipes, but that didn't stop me from seeing you in a completely different way," Disher said. "As a capable police officer."

That shamed me to my core. I felt my skin instantly flush. "You're right. I'm really, really sorry, sir."

38

"That's more like it," he said with a smile.

"I hope you're not going to cry again," Monk said.

"Again?" Disher asked.

"Never mind, sir," I said, hustling Monk out the door. "We need to get back out on patrol. We can't catch crooks in here."

CHAPTER FOUR:
MR. MONK ON THE STREET

Instead of hopping into one of the three
other available squad cars, Monk suggested
that we go on foot patrol up Springfield
Avenue, Summit's main drag, to stretch our
legs and interact with the community.

But Monk hated interacting with the community.

What he meant, but wouldn't admit, was
that he wanted to see Ellen Morse again.

I didn't mind. I enjoyed strolling along
tree-lined Springfield Avenue, which was a
lot like Disneyland's Main Street, U.S.A.,
except the stores here sold goods from
Gucci instead of Goofy and the buildings
were, for the most part, authentic small-
town Americana rather than canny re-
creations.

Morse owned the most unusual store in
town. It was a high-end place even though
its products came entirely from rear ends.
The store was called Poop and Monk's

initial reaction to it was entirely predictable: He was revolted and outraged. He considered Morse the Antichrist.

His feelings about the store hadn't changed but, in a remarkable turn of events, his feelings for Ellen Morse had. That's because she was almost as obsessive-compulsive as he was, especially when it came to cleanliness and order, but she was far more socially well adjusted and didn't share his thousands of phobias, particularly those involving excrement.

Her take on poop was that it was not only a natural part of life but also an integral element in the balance of nature. Balance is very important to Monk, so she had him there. She then appealed to his sense of order.

Here's how she explained it to him:

"Think of poop as a byproduct in the process of manufacturing a product or creating energy. If you do, you'll see it as something left over, a part that no longer fits anywhere, that has to be organized and reintegrated in some way or the natural balance is thrown completely out of whack."

He couldn't argue with that. But he couldn't get past his disgust, either.

Which brings us to that afternoon on Springfield Avenue. He stopped a few yards

41

short of Poop, unable to even look in the window.

"Would you please ask Ellen if she'd like to come out and say hello?" he asked.

"Sure," I said and started for the door.

"Ask her to take a shower first," he said.

I stopped. "That is probably the least romantic thing you could possibly say to her."

"I won't be saying it," he said. "You will."

"No, I won't."

"She'd appreciate it, coming from you," he said.

"No, she wouldn't."

"It's girl talk. Girls talk about showers and grooming activities all the time. She'd take it as sisterly advice."

"I'm not telling her to take a shower before she steps outside."

"At least be sure that she washes her hands," Monk said. "And you might also ask her if she's had a tetanus shot."

"Why would I ask her that?"

"It could come up in conversation."

"That subject has never come up in any conversation I have ever had."

"Having seen your personal grooming habits, I am not surprised but I am alarmed," Monk said. "Have you had a tetanus shot?"

"Yes, I have," I said. "See, that's not so hard. Why don't you ask her?"

"I haven't found the right moment."

"You mean you still haven't asked her if all her vaccinations are up-to-date?"

"I know," he said. "It's reckless and irresponsible of me. But I don't want her to get the wrong idea."

"That you're romantically interested in her."

"I'm not," he said.

"Then why do you want to know if she's been vaccinated?"

"Public health and safety."

I turned my back on him and went to Morse's store, which had a display of coprolites in the window. *Coprolite* is a fancy word for fossilized dinosaur dung, which looks like an ossified pile of soft-serve ice cream. She sold a tiny piece, about the size of one single-scoop cone, for two thousand dollars, which seemed cheap for something sixty-five million years old, even if it was crap. On the other hand, a wristwatch with a coprolite face, also on display in the window, sold for twelve thousand dollars, so there was definitely money to be made in dinosaur droppings.

I walked inside the store. Poop had the ambience of an art gallery crossed with the hippie vibe of a Marin County health food store. The sounds of burbling springs, birdcalls, and the wind rustling the leaves of tall trees played softly from hidden speakers and the air was heavy with floral incense.

Morse was in the stationery aisle, showing a young couple in their twenties her selection of elephant, rhino, and bison dung paper and greeting cards. She had long blond hair, piercing blue eyes, and skin so soft and perfect that it made me half tempted to try out the dung moisturizers from India that she used.

"It's the perfect stationery for a green wedding," Morse told the couple. "You can use it as stock for printing or engraving as you would with any other kind of paper. We also have preprinted, general wedding invitations that you can fill out by hand."

"Cool," the young girl said. "Do you have poop ink?"

"Of course," Morse said, spotting me. "It's at the end of the aisle."

"What about a poop quill?" the young man asked.

"I'm afraid not," Morse said. "Why don't you take a look at the inks while I step outside for a word with Officer Teeger."

The couple both looked at me as Morse came over. I'd seen them around town.

44

They smiled at me and I smiled back. Being able to recognize people in the community was one of the things that appealed to me about Summit.

Morse met me at the door. She was in her forties but could have passed for much younger. She carried herself with a natural grace that I could never pull off, even if Julie Andrews spent a year training me to be a princess.

"I like to think of myself as liberal," I said, low enough to ensure that the couple couldn't hear me, "but I can't help thinking it's a bad omen to send out wedding invitations made of crap."

"The only way the guests will know the paper is made from dung is if the couple chooses to tell them," Morse said. "And if they do, I think they are saying something meaningful about their connection to nature, that their love, and the celebration of their bond, is a beautiful and essential part of the circle of life."

"Wow," I said. "You're good."

"Did Adrian send you in to get me?"

"He did," I said. "He asked me to remind you to wash your hands."

"Good idea. I've handled a lot of money today and you have no idea where it's been or how many dirty hands and grimy pockets it has passed through." She went to the front counter, where there was a bottle of hand sanitizer by the cash register. She squirted a dollop on her hands, rubbed them together, then headed to the door. "You can never be too clean."

No wonder she and Monk got along so well.

We both went outside, where we found Monk writing up a ticket for a man in his thirties wearing a loose-fitting, short-sleeve vintage bowling shirt and cargo shorts. The man had a day's growth of beard and his hair was cut so short that it looked like a shadow on his head. But the style worked for him.

"I'm glad to see you, Officer," the man said to me. "Maybe you can talk some sense into your partner. He's ticketing me for traveling in the wrong lane."

"You're lucky you didn't have a head-on collision with someone," Monk said.

"He's right," I said. "That's a serious moving violation."

"I agree, if you're in your car on the street," the man said. "But not if you're walking on the sidewalk."

"You were still in the wrong lane," Monk said.

"There are no lanes on a sidewalk," the

man said.

"They're invisible," Monk said. "But rest assured, they are there."

I took the ticket book from Monk. "Why don't you let me handle this? You have someone who'd like to have a word with you."

Monk looked back, saw Morse waiting, and nodded. "Okay, but penmanship counts."

He walked over to her and while they talked, I pulled the businessman aside. His driver's license was clipped to Monk's notebook. His name was Stephen Booth. He was thirty-six years old and a resident of Summit.

"We'd appreciate it, Mr. Booth, if you walked on the right side of the sidewalk, just like you would drive on the right side of the road."

"Why?"

"Because it's what most people do, whether they realize it or not."

"I've never noticed," he said.

"You would if you went to London. You know how people there drive on the opposite side of the street? Well, they walk down the sidewalk the same way."

"I didn't know that," he said.

I didn't, either. I'd been to London, but I

couldn't remember if they walked any differently down the sidewalk than we did. But I figured that it sounded plausible.

"So now you know that there are invisible lanes on the sidewalk that we impose on ourselves to reflect the traffic patterns on the street. There's no law that says you have to follow them, but I'm sure Officer Monk isn't the only one who'd like it if you did."

"Would you like it?"

"Yes, I would."

He smiled and he got these little laugh lines in his cheeks that made him look like a mischievous child. "Then I'll do it and think of you every time I do."

"You're flirting with me," I said.

"I'm glad you noticed," he said.

"I'm an officer of the law. I'm very observant." I smiled and handed him back his license. "I'll let you off with a stern warning this time, Mr. Booth."

"Please call me Steve. Perhaps I could thank you with a cup of coffee?"

I glanced back at Monk, who appeared to be finishing up his conversation with Morse.

"That would be nice. But it will have to be some other time."

"It's an open invitation. I have lunch most days at the Buttercup Pantry," he said, gesturing to the café right next door. "You're

48

always welcome at my table."

"Thank you," I said. "I'll be sure to stop by one of these days."

"I hope you'll make it soon" — he glanced at the name tag on my chest — "Officer Teeger."

"Natalie," I said.

"Natalie," he said and walked away. I watched him go and then I tore the ticket out of Monk's notebook and stuck it into my pocket so I had Booth's contact information for safekeeping. He would be my first date when I officially moved to Summit.

Actually, he'd be my first date in months anywhere. But I'd be on my guard. I might even bring my gun.

That was because my taste in men lately hadn't been so good. The last couple of guys that I'd dated turned out to be killers, which is enough to make any woman wary of romance.

Or make her enter a nunnery.

But I still had a pulse and the desires that went with it, so I wasn't ready to give up on love altogether.

When I turned around, Morse was heading back into her store and Monk was coming my way.

"Did you ticket him?" Monk asked.

"Yes," I said. "But I made it a warning

citation rather than a violation. I think we scared him straight."

"Good," Monk said. "I believe we're making a real difference in this community."

"So do I," I said and I meant it, too.

CHAPTER FIVE:
MR. MONK GETS
AN INVITATION

It was our last night in town before our flight back to San Francisco, where we would have three weeks to prepare for our big move east.

Monk went to dinner at Morse's house while I shared Chinese takeout with Sharona and Disher at their kitchen table. It was a rare pleasure, since Monk refused to share entrées and for me that was half the fun of eating Chinese food.

Disher quickly wolfed down his dinner. He had only a few minutes to spare before having to attend a city council meeting. It probably would have been less hassle for him if he'd had a quick bite at the office, but he thought it was important to come home and see Sharona, even if it was for only a few minutes over chow mein and kung pao pork.

That said a lot to me about Disher and how he felt about Sharona. He was a good man and she was lucky to have him.

After he left, Sharona got out a carton of Oreo Cookie ice cream and brought it and two spoons to the table. It was an evil, wretched thing to do and I loved her for it.

Outwardly, Sharona and I were very different. I was a California girl, casually dressed and sun-kissed. Sharona was loudly, aggressively, and proudly a child of New Jersey. Everything about the way she walked, talked, and dressed reinforced every cliché about women from that state.

My style in clothes was loose and casual. I didn't show much skin, though I was hardly a prude. I just didn't like men leering at me. Don't get me wrong. It's not that I thought I had a spectacular body that would drive men wild if they got a peek at it. Men will leer at the slightest hint of cleavage, which is all I can muster anyway.

Sharona dressed tight and flashy, with skirts as short and necklines as low as she could find. She thought she was hot and liked it when men stared at her. And they did. So did most women. She wore a push-up bra that shoved her boobs in her nose, not to mention everybody else's.

I used very little makeup, only enough to hide my flaws and accentuate my strengths. But Sharona used a lot, highlighting everything, using color like pinpoint halogens so that nobody would ever miss her face in a crowd.

I had short hair that I didn't do much with, and I had no desire to change that. She had big hair that she twisted, shaped, colored, teased, curled, streaked, and extended in all kinds of ways.

But below the surface we were a lot alike.

We were both strong willed, fiercely independent, and ready to fight for what we believed in. We'd both been single mothers with limited incomes, so we knew how to survive and how to stretch a dollar. And we'd both worked for Adrian Monk and cared deeply for him, despite the misery he caused us.

We probably understood each other better than anyone else could.

So it was no surprise that she sensed my anxiety about my trip home and brought out the ice cream.

I stuck my spoon in and helped myself to a big scoop.

"I know what it's like to move across the country and start a new life," Sharona said. "Just thinking about all the things you have to do is so emotionally overwhelming you almost feel paralyzed."

I swallowed my ice cream and went for

another scoop. "Is it that obvious?"

"It's only natural," she said. "I've done it four times and it's never any easier. But once the actual move is over and things settle down, I'm always grateful that I took the risk and made the change. You have one advantage, though, that I never had."

"What's that?"

"Me," she said, taking a spoonful of ice cream herself. "Someone who has already been down the road you're traveling. I've got your back. I'll start by looking for your new place here while you're settling your affairs in San Francisco."

"You make it sound like I'm going back for a funeral," I said. "Come to think of it, I am. I'm burying my old life."

"Oh, stop being so melodramatic," she said, carefully exposing and removing a big chunk of cookie, like an archaeologist finding a rare fossil. "You're making a change, that's all."

"I'm beginning to understand why Mr. Monk hates change so much."

"Don't you love your new job?"

"I do," I said. "Even the mundane stuff is a thrill for me."

"Don't you like Summit?"

"I do," I said. "I feel very comfortable here."

"So you should be excited about what's ahead."

"I am," I said. "But it's not as simple as that."

"Of course it is," she said.

"For the last twenty-plus years, my life has been in San Francisco," I said. "It's where I married Mitch, bought a house, and raised Julie."

Sharona waved away my argument. "Your husband has been dead for over a decade. Stop using him as an excuse not to have a life."

"It's more than that. How is Julie going to feel about me moving to Summit to become a cop?"

"Doesn't she know that you're already working here?"

"She knows that Mr. Monk and I are here helping Randy out," I said. "But I haven't told her that I'm actually working as a police officer."

"Or that you've already accepted Randy's job offer."

"This is big stuff. I need to tell her face-to-face," I said. "I don't want her to be hurt."

"What does she have to be hurt about?"

"That I made the decision without consulting her, for one thing."

55

"It's your life," Sharona said. "Not hers. You don't have to consult anyone."

"I'm being selfish," I said. "I'm abandoning her and our life together."

"I've got a news bulletin for you, honey. Julie is an adult. She's got a life of her own now, apart from yours. And I'll bet that she's not calling you to consult on every decision that she makes."

"I wish she would," I said.

"You should follow her example. You aren't responsible for raising a child anymore. You have your life back. You can do as you please without anyone or anything tying you down. There are a lot of people who'd envy the opportunity that you have now to reinvent yourself."

"But I'll be leaving our house behind, the one thing Julie and I both have left that we shared with Mitch," I said. "How can I do that?"

"She did," Sharona said.

"She left to go to college, but it wasn't like she went all the way to, oh, Summit, New Jersey. She went across the bay to Berkeley. She knew that she could always come home," I said. "Where will home be now?"

"The one she makes for herself. It's just a house and San Francisco is just a city. It's

56

the memories that matter and they're going with you."

"But the San Francisco Bay Area is where Mr. Monk has lived his entire life."

"And Adrian is coming here, too. That alone should tell you something."

"But what if he changes his mind and decides to stay in San Francisco?"

"Ah, now we're getting to the heart of it." Sharona got up, went to the cupboard, took out a package of Oreo cookies, and set it on the table. "You're afraid to leave him."

"He needs me, Sharona," I said.

"Sure he does." She opened the package, took out some cookies, and dropped them into the container of Oreo Cookie ice cream. "But does he need you as much as you need him?"

She began to mash the cookies into the ice cream with her spoon. I could see why she'd brought out the extra Oreos. I'd need the reinforcement. This was heavy stuff.

"Mr. Monk has come a long way in the last few years," I said. "I'm sure he's capable now of living on his own. But I worry that if there isn't someone running interference for him, cutting down on the little distractions and smoothing out his misunderstandings with others, then the frustration, confusion, and fear could build up in him,

57

become too much, and he could crack."

"He could," she said. She stopped mashing and took a big cookie-filled scoop for herself. "But it's not your problem."

"Easy for you to say," I said before I dug out a spoonful of ice cream and stuffed it in my mouth. It was delicious. Pure Oreo heaven.

"Do you think it was easy for me to leave Adrian?" she said. "He was much less capable of taking care of himself back then than he is now. But one thing was true then and is still true today: Adrian becomes your life and pretty soon you forget you have one of your own. I knew if I didn't go, I'd end up sacrificing my life and my happiness for his and I wasn't willing to do that. But I also knew I couldn't face walking out on him. So one day I just didn't show up. I left without even saying good-bye. And you know what? He survived. He found you."

"What if he doesn't find someone else?"

"I think he already has," she said.

As if on cue, that's when Monk returned from his dinner date and walked in on us in the kitchen.

"Are you two drunk?" Monk asked.

"No, of course not," I said. "What makes you say that?"

"Because that's the only thing that could

explain such reckless and unsanitary behavior," Monk said.

"There's nothing wrong with sharing ice cream, Adrian," Sharona said.

"Did you both floss and brush your teeth before eating out of the same container of ice cream?"

"No," I said.

"So what you're actually sharing is ice cream slathered with hot saliva teeming with millions of germs, bits of undigested food, and flecks of plaque. I hope you're not thinking of putting that massive petri dish in the freezer and preserving it. That's how the Black Death started."

"With Oreo Cookie ice cream?" I said. "Did they even have Oreos back then?"

"Relax, Adrian," Sharona said. "We intend to finish it here and now and with no regrets."

"I'll be sure to quote that in your eulogies," Monk said and went to the refrigerator to get himself a bottle of Fiji water. He cleaned the top with a disinfectant wipe, then unscrewed the cap and drank directly from the bottle.

"Rough night?" Sharona asked.

"I told Ellen that I needed to find a place to live," Monk said.

"And that made you feel anxious," Sharona said. "Don't worry, Adrian. While you're in San Francisco, I'll start looking for first-floor apartments that are even numbered, symmetrical, and spotlessly clean."

"She pointed out that her house has four bedrooms, two baths, and was extremely clean and symmetrical," Monk said.

"That's true," I said. "It's got the same disinfected operating-room smell as your place."

"She offered me a room in her house for as long as I wanted," Monk said.

I shared a look with Sharona. "What did you say?"

"Naturally, I declined," Monk said.

"Because you're not ready for that kind of commitment," Sharona said. "And everything that it implies."

"It's not the rental agreement that concerns me," Monk said.

"She was asking you to live with her, Adrian," Sharona said.

"Strictly as a tenant," Monk said.

"No, she wasn't," I said. "She wants to be with you, Mr. Monk."

"I'm sure you're mistaken," Monk said. "She's not that kind of woman."

"Then why did you say no?" Sharona asked.

"Because I can't live in the same house with someone who collects excrement art and uses excrement products."

"It hasn't stopped you from spending every free minute you have with her at her house," I said.

"That's because she put her personal excrement collection in hiding and refrained from using products derived from excrement while I was around," Monk said. "But it's still there. She still engages in excremental conduct. It's the elephant excrement in the room we don't talk about."

"So what did you tell her?" I asked.

"That I'd be living with you," Monk said.

"But you won't be," I said.

He raised his eyebrows. "Of course I will."

"Let me make this perfectly clear," I said. "I will never share a home with you. Here or anywhere else."

"Why not?" he asked.

"Because I have a life of my own," I said.

"That revolves entirely around me," Monk said. "Think how much easier it will be once we're living in the same house."

Sharona looked at me triumphantly. "I rest my case."

61

Chapter Six:
Mr. Monk Goes Home

Disher drove us to Newark Airport in the morning for our flight back home. Before we got out of the Suburban, he handed us leather wallets containing our badges.

"You may be going back to San Francisco," he said, "but you're still Summit police officers."

It was a very shrewd move on his part, a way to make sure we didn't get too comfortable back home and begin to second-guess our decisions to make our temporary jobs permanent.

It also played on his understanding of our histories and vulnerabilities. Monk had fought for years to get reinstated to the SFPD after being thrown off for psychological reasons following his wife's murder. Now Disher was showing his confidence in Monk by handing him a badge without making him struggle to earn it.

I'd bounced around for years, doing all

kinds of jobs, before I stumbled into the role of Monk's assistant. Even so, I wasn't sure if I had any real, marketable skills or if I'd made any meaningful contributions to his investigations. Only recently had I begun to think that police work was something that I might not only have an affinity for, but might actually enjoy doing. By handing me a badge, Disher was officially recognizing my abilities. It was like the Wizard of Oz proving the Scarecrow had a brain by giving him a diploma.

We didn't have any luggage, since our belongings had burned in a hotel fire (which is another story), so we checked in at one of the computer terminals and made our way to the gate.

Monk brought plastic booties to wear on his feet when he went through security without his shoes, and he didn't object to walking through the X-ray machine this time.

Perhaps it was because he felt a kinship with the TSA agents. When they saw our badges, they asked us if we had any weapons to declare, and I said just my hands. I think they thought I was serious. They seemed to treat us with a deference reserved for law enforcement officers and Monk wasn't going to jeopardize that by making any kind of scene.

One of Monk's big phobias is flying. Usually, the only way to get him on a plane for a long flight is to give him an experimental drug that diminishes his OCD but turns him into a jerk. The other is to slip him a mickey, which is what we did to get him out to New Jersey. Much to my surprise, and despite his fury about being drugged before, he actually requested a strong sedative before getting on the flight. Once again, I credit the badge.

So while Monk slept through most of the five-hour flight, I sat in quiet contemplation, thinking about the tumultuous changes I was about to make in my life. After weeks of sleeping on Disher's couch, I was looking forward to my own bed and the comforts of my own home, one I was about to abandon for a new career on the other side of the country.

As a cop.

Officer Natalie Teeger.

Wow.

It was hard to believe, but I had the evidence right there in my hands.

My badge.

I spent hours staring at the badge and appreciating what it represented about me and what it promised for my future.

I also had to admire once again how clever Disher was to give us those badges. Up until then, I'd never thought of him as being that smart or manipulative. Then again, I never saw him as chief-of-police material, either. I was obviously a lousy judge of character.

I wasn't looking forward to packing up and saying good-bye to everyone, and yet I was eager to see how my parents, my daughter, Julie, and Captain Leland Stottlemeyer — Monk's oldest friend and our boss at the SFPD — would all react to my badge.

We arrived at San Francisco International Airport in the early evening and I led a stumbling, very groggy Monk to my car in the long-term parking lot.

It's a good thing that Monk was practically sleepwalking, because if he'd been alert and had seen the thick layer of dirt and bird crap on my car, he would not have gotten in, and would probably have called the Department of Health. Lucky for us both, he fell asleep moments after I sat him down and buckled him in.

I paid the attendant at the exit booth a parking fee roughly equal to the Kelley Blue Book value of my car, an expense that Disher would reimburse, and drove us into the city.

I hadn't taken a sleeping pill and yet there

was a dreamlike quality to the drive. All the passing scenery was familiar, but I felt removed from what I was seeing, as if it were already a memory.

San Francisco was the same as it was when I left it, but I didn't return as the same person I was before. I'd changed in fundamental ways, and not just because I had a badge in my pocket.

While I was in Summit, I shot a man in the line of duty. I did so without the slightest hesitation. He'd survived and I felt no remorse for my quick action. It wasn't just pulling the trigger that changed me — it was the knowledge that I *could* and that I *would*.

It surprised me. And I knew I'd be making more discoveries about myself in the coming months. It was scary and exciting at the same time.

I glanced over at Monk and wondered if, when he wasn't sedated, he was feeling the same mix of excitement and anxiety that I was. Then again, feeling anxious was his usual state of mind.

I pulled up to his Art Deco–style apartment building on Pine, a shrinking pocket of affordability tucked between the old money and Victorian mansions of Pacific Heights to the north and the new money

66

that was gentrifying the Western District to the south.

I walked him to his door, opened it for him, and then led him all the way in to his bed. He collapsed facefirst on his comforter. I took off his shoes, but beyond that, I left him as he was. If I so much as removed his jacket, he'd be humiliated and outraged when he woke up.

Most homes that have been closed up for weeks smell musty and stale, but not Monk's place. It smelled as if it had just been thoroughly cleaned. I credited that inexplicable freshness to the accumulation of disinfectants and cleansers over the years. I was certain that I could bottle the air in his apartment and use it to disinfect operating rooms. On my way out, I checked a few tabletops and shelves and couldn't find even a particle of dust.

But I was sure that when Monk awoke he would survey the apartment and decide it was caked in filth and nearly uninhabitable. At least it would make moving out easier for him to accept.

I slipped away, locked the door behind me, and headed south on Divisadero, across Market Street, and into Noe Valley, the quirky, self-consciously bohemian neighborhood where I lived on a tree-lined street of

Victorian row houses, most of which were occupied by young families with lots of kids and dogs and credit card debt.

I parked in the driveway and immediately felt the emotional tug of home. I fought the urge to run to the door and, instead, walked slowly across the grass and up the steps of my front porch to appreciate my little piece of San Francisco real estate.

I unlocked the door and turned on the lights as I stepped inside. My house didn't smell musty and stale, as I was expecting it to. Instead, it smelled like pizza, which was odd, since I couldn't remember having one before I left.

Not only that, but there were two empty beer bottles on the coffee table.

And I don't drink beer.

That left only one inescapable conclusion. *Someone has been living in my house.*

My first thought was that Julie had used my house to party while I was away and, since she didn't have any warning that I was returning, hadn't had a chance to clean up the evidence.

I didn't see her car out front, but just in case she and some boyfriend were in the house in the middle of something I didn't want to walk in on, I announced my arrival.

"Julie, I'm home."

I was standing there, waiting for a reply, or for some sound of movement, when I noticed something else unusual.

All the family photos of me, Julie, and Mitch were gone from the walls and bookshelves.

Why would Julie remove those?

She wouldn't.

Something wasn't right. I reached for the gun I didn't have in the holster I wasn't wearing. Since I had no weapon, I dropped my purse and grabbed an umbrella from the stand by the door. Hefting it like a batter waiting for a pitch, I moved slowly into the kitchen.

The table was set for a breakfast for two. There was an assortment of cereal boxes and jams, two cups of coffee, a carton of milk, a mushy bowl of cut watermelon, and a plate of dry toast.

Someone has been living in my house.

There was a pizza carton on the kitchen counter, four empty wine bottles in the recycle bin, and the dish rack was full of clean dishes.

Someone has been eating my food.

At least whoever it was had the courtesy to wash my dishes. So why did he leave the empty bottles in the living room and the untouched breakfast on the table?

I left the kitchen and crept down the dark hall toward my bedroom, cursing the old floorboards for creaking under my feet. The bedroom door was ajar. I used my foot to slowly open the door.

There was a pair of red-soled Christian Louboutin high-heeled shoes, a Chanel silk blouse, a short skirt, a lacy bra, and G-string panties.

They certainly weren't my clothes or my daughter's. The shoes alone cost more than Julie's tuition.

The discarded clothing made a trail to the bed, where the sheets and comforter were a rumpled mess.

Someone has been sleeping in my bed.

As I stepped into the room, I heard water dripping behind me. I turned around and headed toward the half-open bathroom door down the hall, midway between my room and Julie's old bedroom.

But that's when I picked up a metallic odor in the air that stopped me cold, my heart thumping hard and heavy in my chest.

I recognized the smell.

And, in a way I was thankful for it, because it gave me a warning and a moment to prepare for the horror I was going to see.

It was the smell of blood.

Gobs of it.

I'd never been more afraid in my life.

I held my breath, my heartbeat resonating through my whole rigid body, and with a shaking hand, I used the tip of the umbrella to ease open the bathroom door.

The first thing I saw was the puddle of blood and water on the linoleum.

And then I saw the pale female arm draped over the side of the tub, crimson water spilling over the edge, a bloody straight razor dangling from her hand.

And then I saw the naked red-haired woman sitting in the tub, her head lolled back against the white tile wall and staring at me with wide, dead eyes, her throat slit open in an obscene smile.

I took a sudden breath, as sharp and painful as a knife, and fell to my knees, my body racked by deep, gut-wrenching sobs.

Of profound relief.

There was a dead woman in my bathtub.

And it wasn't my daughter.

71

CHAPTER SEVEN:
MR. MONK HAS A DREAM

I got a grip on myself, stood up, and backed out of the room. I retraced my steps through the house, dropped the umbrella back in the stand, and grabbed my purse on my way out the front door.

I sat down on the porch, took in a few deep breaths, then got some tissues out of my purse, wiped my eyes and blew my nose.

An attractive young couple walked by, pushing a stroller. They smiled and waved and I smiled and waved back at them as if I were one of those nice neighbors who didn't have a dead naked woman in my bathtub. It made me wonder what might be hidden behind the smiles and draped windows of my neighbors.

I reached into my purse, took out my cell phone, and called Captain Stottlemeyer. He answered on the first ring.

"Hey, Captain, it's Natalie."

"How are things in Summit?"

"I'm here in San Francisco," I said.

"It's about time. I was beginning to wonder if you and Monk were ever coming home," he said. "When did you get back?"

"I just walked in the door," I said.

"And Monk insisted that you alert me right away that he's ready and available for work," Stottlemeyer said. "Consider me alerted. Now get some rest. I'll be sure to light up the bat signal as soon as there's a tricky murder I need his help with."

"Actually, Mr. Monk didn't ask me to call. He's at home in bed. He took a sleeping pill before we got on the plane and probably doesn't even realize that he's in San Francisco yet. So he's going to be a bit disoriented once you manage to wake him up."

"Why would I want to do that?"

"Because you'll want to stop by and get him tonight on your way over to my house."

"As eager as I am to hear all about your trip," he said, "I think I can wait a few days until you get settled in."

"Yeah, but by then the corpse in my bathtub will have decomposed so much, the neighbors will be complaining about the smell."

There was a long moment of silence. "There's a dead body in your bathtub?"

73

"There is," I said.

"Who is it?"

"I don't know," I said. "I came home from the airport and there she was, naked with her throat slit, sitting in a tub full of water. From what I can tell, she's been there since this morning."

"Did you touch anything?"

"Just the front door and an umbrella," I said. "As soon as I saw the body, I retraced my steps and went back outside. But it's my house, so my fingerprints are going to be everywhere anyway. I am now out front, securing the crime scene."

"Okay, sit tight. Someone will be there within five minutes. I'll be there shortly with Monk. Are you going to be okay until then?"

"It's not the first time I've seen a murder victim. It's not even the first time I've seen one in my house."

"That may be the most depressing thing I've heard all day," he said.

"The day isn't over yet," I said.

Two squad cars showed up a few minutes after my call and four officers got out. I identified myself and remained on the porch with one of the officers while the others got to work. One went into the backyard to secure the back door of the house, another established a perimeter with crime scene tape, and the last posted himself on the street to keep the curious neighbors away.

The medical examiner, the forensics team, and Lieutenant Amy Devlin arrived at about the same time, nearly causing a pileup. But Devlin won out, cutting off the other vehicles and skidding to a stop at the curb in her 1990 Firebird.

She slammed her door and marched up the front walk toward me.

"Welcome home," Devlin said. "Do you really have a stiff in your bathroom?"

"I'm afraid so," I said.

Devlin wore her standard uniform — blue jeans, a T-shirt, and a leather jacket that looked like it had been salvaged from a fire and attacked with the same weed whacker she used to style her hair. Her badge was clipped to her belt right beside her gun, which I bet she even wore with a bathing suit.

"Anybody you know?"

"Nope," I said, hoping she didn't plan on asking me every question that I'd already answered for the captain.

The forensic team and Dr. Daniel Hetzer, the medical examiner, went past us on their way into the house. I'd met Hetzer a few times before. He was a balding man who carefully maintained two days' worth of stubble on his face as if the hair were a rare orchid. I acknowledged him with a nod, and he nodded back at me, which provoked a glower of irritation from Devlin, who'd only recently transferred over to replace Disher. She resented my familiarity with everyone in homicide, especially while she was still finding her footing.

"Did you have anyone taking care of your house or picking up your mail while you were away?" she asked.

"The gardener comes once a week and mows the lawn, but that's it," I replied. "I put a vacation hold on my mail and newspaper."

"Who has keys to your house?"

"Just me and my daughter."

"Where is she?"

I shrugged. "At her apartment in Berkeley, I suppose. I haven't called her yet."

"Could the dead woman be one of her friends?"

"This woman looks older," I said. "I peg her to be in her late twenties, early thirties."

"That doesn't mean your daughter didn't befriend her, give her a key, and let her crash at your place while you were away," Devlin said.

"That's true," I said. "But Julie wouldn't

do that."

Devlin started toward the front door and I followed her. She stopped at the door and turned to me.

"Where do you think you're going?" she asked.

"Into my house," I replied.

"It's a crime scene."

"I'm aware of that."

"That means it's cops only inside until the captain decides it's okay for civilians to come in."

"No problem," I said and flashed her my badge. "I suggest you get some booties on your shoes before you go inside. I don't want you contaminating our crime scene by tracking in stuff from your car."

"Let me see that." Devlin gestured to my badge and I handed it to her. She examined it closely. I thought she might even bite it to see if it was metal instead of tinfoil. "How many rings did you have to toss to win this at the county fair?"

"It's authentic," I said and pointed to the Summit Police photo ID on the opposite flap of the badge wallet. "I'm a police officer now. I'm only here long enough to settle my affairs, then I'm going back east."

"They'll give these to anybody these days." She tossed the badge wallet back to me. "Are you taking Monk with you?"

"That's the plan," I said.

"At least there's a bright side to this." She shouldered past me and headed over to the CSI van, where she helped herself to plastic booties from a box by the door.

I'd thought that after all Devlin and I had been through together, I'd proven myself as reasonably competent and we'd finally worked through her hostility toward me and Monk.

Apparently I was wrong.

I marched up to her. "You looked at my badge like it's a personal insult."

"It is," she said.

"Whether you like it or not, it means I am a cop now," I said. "Just like you."

"You're nothing like me," she said as she slipped the booties over her shoes. "You haven't been through the Academy, you haven't put in years walking a beat, you haven't spent months at a time undercover where the slightest mistake could put you in the ground. You're a dilettante."

We'd been through variations of this dance many times before and I was tired of it. The difference now was that I had a badge, and while I could see how that might add some salt to her perceived wounds, it also gave me an advantage I didn't have before.

I reached for a set of booties from the van and tugged them over my shoes.

"What you think of me or of my experience doesn't matter, because as far as the law or anybody else is concerned, my badge makes me as much a cop as yours makes you."

"Except that I'm a homicide detective, you're a patrol officer, and you're thousands of miles outside of your itty-bitty jurisdiction. So your badge might as well have come from a cereal box for all it's worth here."

I stepped in front of her and looked her right in the eye. "I'm tired, I'm jet-lagged, and there's a dead body in my bathroom. I don't have the patience to argue with you, so listen up. I'm a cop and that's my house. I don't need your permission to go inside. You, on the other hand, need mine. So shove the attitude or you'll stay here directing traffic while I begin the investigation."

She took a step toward me. We were so close that our noses were almost touching. "You try to get between me and that house and I will take you down so hard you'll think you were hit by a bus."

And that's how we were standing when Stottlemeyer and Monk approached us. We were so caught up in our contest measuring a particular part of the male anatomy that neither of us possessed that we hadn't heard them drive up and get out of the car.

Whatever hostility I felt toward Devlin evaporated when I saw Stottlemeyer. I felt a wave of affection for him. He was his usual rumpled, weary self, his bushy mustache in need of a trim, his clothes wrinkled, his tie loosely knotted at his neck. I'd missed him.

"I see you two are as chummy as ever," Stottlemeyer said to the two of us.

Devlin and I, suddenly both self-conscious, took a big step back from each other.

I looked over at Monk, who was glassy-eyed and a bit wobbly on his feet.

"Are you okay, Mr. Monk?" I asked.

"I'm just a little sleepy. The captain woke me up from a nap," Monk said. "You wouldn't believe the dream I had. It was so vivid. You were in it. So were Sharona and Randy. And a lady who sold poo. We were police officers."

"That wasn't a dream," I said. "That really happened."

"We were really police officers? In Summit, New Jersey?"

"Yes, we were. We still are." I showed Monk my badge. "You've got one, too."

Stottlemeyer raised his eyebrows in surprise. "Randy let you keep them?"

I wasn't ready to answer the question yet so I ignored it.

Monk took his badge out of his pocket and stared at it like it was the spinning top totem that Leonardo DiCaprio kept around in *Inception* to remind him of what was real and what was not.

"What about the poo lady?" Monk asked.

"Ellen Morse. Her store is called Poop. You had dinner with her last night."

"She really sells crap?" Stottlemeyer asked me.

I nodded. "Stuff like fossilized dinosaur dung and an array of artwork and products made from excrement, like cooking oil made from goat droppings, coffee made from civet poop, and shampoo made from cow patties. She caters to a very wealthy and discerning clientele."

"And Monk ate with her?" Stottlemeyer said.

"Often," I said. "He likes her."

"Maybe I'm the one who's dreaming." Stottlemeyer lowered his head and massaged his brow. "Or having a stroke."

Devlin cleared her throat. "I hate to intrude on this touching reunion, but there's a corpse in the bathtub and it's getting ripe.

81

Maybe we should go inside and start processing the crime scene."

Monk blinked hard, suddenly alert, like a bloodhound picking up a scent, and pinned Devlin with his gaze.

"You're not going in Natalie's house wearing that," Monk said to her.

"Wearing what?" Devlin said, checking herself out.

"That leather jacket," Monk said.

Stottlemeyer looked up at him. "I know you've never liked the idea of people wearing animal hides or upholstering their furniture with them, but I thought you'd made peace with it a long time ago."

"That was before Ellen told me how they tan leather," Monk said. "They soak the hide in a mixture of wood ashes and urine to make it easier to scrape off the fibers and then, in a process called bating, they soak it in a vat of hot dung, gathered from dogs and other carnivores. The dung has an enzyme that breaks down the collagen in the hide and gives it a soft, supple texture. So basically, Lieutenant Devlin, you're wearing a latrine."

Devlin groaned with irritation, took off her jacket, and tossed it on the hood of her Firebird. "Happy now?"

"It would be better if you incinerated it."

82

"Now *that's* the Adrian Monk I know." Stottlemeyer smiled with relief and clapped Monk on the back. "Let's go solve a murder."

CHAPTER EIGHT:
MR. MONK AND GOLDILOCKS

As soon as we stepped into the house, Monk
held his hands out in front of him, as if feeling the heat from a campfire, and began
moving around the living room like a skater,
swaying and dipping and spinning. Stottlemeyer called it Monk Zen, but whatever it
was, it seemed to be his method for identify-
ing patterns and spotting things that were
out of place.

"My family photos have been taken
down," I said, trying to be helpful. "It leads
me to believe that the lady in the tub
wanted to trick someone into thinking that
she lived here."

"That's a good observation," Stottlemeyer
said.

Devlin rolled her eyes. "Positively brilliant.
I'll see you in the bathroom."

She walked away from us. Neither the
captain nor Monk seemed in a big hurry to
get to the corpse. I'd rarely been with the

captain when he first arrived at a crime scene, so I was studying him to pick up his method, which at the moment seemed to be keeping his eye on Monk.

"Was the front door locked when you got here?" Stottlemeyer asked me.

"Yes," I said. "Dead bolt and all."

But the question gave me a thought. I hurried into the kitchen.

"I don't see any signs of a break-in, but this isn't exactly Fort Knox," Stottlemeyer said, trailing after me. "What are you looking for?"

Using a dish glove, I opened my junk drawer, which was filled with stuff like rubber bands, paper clips, loose keys, duct tape, screwdrivers, coupons, batteries, pliers, screws, stamps, nail clippers, and dozens of those L-shaped little hex wrenches from the assemble-it-yourself stuff I bought at Ikea.

"My spare house key," I said. "It's not here. She might have picked the lock or broken in to start with, but it looks like she may have used my keys to come and go after that."

"Somebody did lock up after killing her," Stottlemeyer said. "Whoever it was might have taken the key."

"Looks like I'll be changing the locks when this is all over," I said.

Monk circled the kitchen, studying the table, the counters, and the dishes in the drainer.

"The dishes and utensils that were used indicate that there was only one person staying here," Monk said. "Perhaps for two or three days."

"So she invited someone here for dinner. Perhaps he even stayed for breakfast," Stottlemeyer said. "And then he killed her."

"But why was she in my home and not her own?" I asked. "And how did she know that I, or Julie, or a house sitter, wouldn't walk in on her while she was here?"

"All very good questions," Stottlemeyer said and glanced at Monk. "Got answers for them yet?"

"No, I don't," Monk said.

"It must be the jet lag," Stottlemeyer said. "I think it's time we got a look at Goldilocks."

He headed down the hall. Monk and I followed, passing my bedroom, where Devlin was crouched on the floor, going through a Gucci purse that certainly wasn't mine and that I hadn't initially spotted when I was in there before.

Since the bathroom was small, Stottlemeyer remained in the hallway so as not to crowd the female CSI, who was bagging the razor, and Dr. Hetzer, who crouched beside the tub examining the dead woman.

"What can you tell us, Doc?" Stottlemeyer asked.

"It appears she bled out from the wounds to her neck and wrist, but I can't be sure there aren't other injuries until I've drained the water," he said. "I won't be able to determine the exact cause of death, or other contributory factors, until I get her on a table and open her up."

"She looks pretty opened up to me already," Stottlemeyer said.

"A straight razor will do that," Hetzer said.

His comment made me take a second look at the razor, which was in a baggie in the CSI's hand. I spoke to her.

"Could you please open the bottom drawer of the vanity?"

She looked at Captain Stottlemeyer for approval and he nodded. She opened the drawer, which was where I kept Mitch's old shaving stuff. A key item was missing.

"That was my husband's straight razor," I said. "He liked to shave the old-fashioned way. I kept his shaving kit after he died."

That wasn't entirely the truth. I'd had them since he was deployed to Kosovo. It was what I did every time he was on a mission. It was my way of keeping his presence in the house. The shaving tools and the smell of the cream that still lingered on them reminded me of him.

But in those first agonizing months after he was shot down, leaving me a widowed mother with a small child, they took on added poignancy. I'd take out his shaving brush and run it along my tear-streaked cheeks. It was almost as if he were there, tenderly stroking my face, comforting me and assuring me that we'd get through his loss.

It was bad enough that someone had broken into my home, but for her to have been killed with Mitch's razor felt like sacrilege.

"We'll have to hold on to the razor for a while," Stottlemeyer said.

"I know," I replied.

Monk squeezed between us, leaned into the bathroom, and cocked his head so he could look at the dead woman.

"This wasn't a murder," Monk said. "It was a suicide."

"Or a murder made to look like a suicide," Stottlemeyer said.

Monk shook his head. "The razor is in her right hand. The depth and arc of the wound on her throat are consistent with a self-inflicted lesion."

Dr. Hetzer squinted at the wound. "I've got to agree with Monk on that."

"There also isn't the blood splatter on the wall or splashed water on the floor that would indicate that a struggle took place," Monk said.

"The killer could have cleaned it up," Stottlemeyer said.

"And taken the blood-and water-soaked rags with him?" Monk said, turning to me. "Do you appear to be missing any towels?"

"Not in here," I said. "But I'd have to take a look in my linen closet to be sure. I don't own many towels, so it'll only take me a minute to do an inventory."

I went to the hall closet and checked the towels. They were all accounted for.

"This could all be staged," Stottlemeyer said. "Maybe he killed her somewhere else and put her in the tub afterward."

"But if he killed her elsewhere in the house, where's the blood?" I said. "My carpets are clean."

"I wouldn't go that far," Monk said. "Looking at them is probably what pushed her over the edge."

"Let me get this straight," I said. "You're saying that seeing my dirty carpets drove her to suicide?"

"It's certainly occurred to me more than

once," Monk said. "Seeing those permanent stains can't help but drive you to despair and force you to confront the futility of your own existence."

"Slashing your throat is an awfully brutal way to kill yourself," I said. "Why not take pills? Or slit both of your wrists?"

"Maybe she wanted to be absolutely sure she got the job done," Stottlemeyer said. "Or maybe she wasn't just depressed with her life, she actually hated herself, and those other ways were too gentle a way to go."

"If that's true," I said, "what could she have done that made her feel so angry about who she was?"

"I know what you mean," Monk said. "It's not like she's the one who stained the carpets."

"That wasn't what I was getting at," I said.

Devlin stepped out of the bedroom, holding a wallet. "The victim is Michelle Keeling, age twenty-six, from Las Vegas, Nevada. Does that ring any bells?"

"Never heard of her," I said. "And I certainly didn't invite her to house-sit and kill herself in my bathroom."

Stottlemeyer gestured to the purse. "Find anything else in her purse?"

"Come see for yourself," Devlin said and led us back into my bedroom. She had the contents of the purse spread out on the bed, already placed in transparent evidence bags.

The first thing I noticed was that my spare house keys weren't among the stuff in her purse. The second thing I noticed was a baggie full of jewelry.

"That's my wedding ring," I said, picking up the bag. "And the rest of my jewelry. She even took Mitch's old watch and cuff links."

"So she was a squatter and a thief," Monk said.

"But not a very picky one," I said. "This stuff is hardly worth stealing. Even if you melted my wedding ring down, it wouldn't be worth more than a few hundred dollars. The only real value any of this has is sentimental."

"How sentimental are you about this?" Devlin picked up a baggie containing a stack of crisp hundred-dollar bills that had to add up to a few thousand dollars.

"I work for Adrian Monk," I said. "I don't have that kind of money around the house. Or anywhere else."

Monk gestured to the pillows. "Two people slept in this bed. You can see that from the pillows and the way the bottom sheet is wrinkled. Whoever the other person was suffers from acid reflux disease."

"How can you tell?" Devlin asked.

"The pillows are stacked so that he could sleep with his upper body raised," Monk said. "And there's a Pepcid tablet on the floor between the bed and the nightstand. Natalie doesn't take Pepcids."

"This is true," I said.

Devlin took a baggie and picked up the pill with it. "So we're looking for a killer with heartburn."

Stottlemeyer examined an evidence bag containing a few matchbooks from Keeling's purse. "It appears that Michelle liked to visit the Belmont Hotel bar. She'd need all that cash just to buy a Diet Coke there."

I knew the Belmont. Everyone did. It was built after the great San Francisco earthquake in the heart of Union Square and had become a local landmark. I glanced down at her clothes and, based on what they cost, and the money in her purse, she'd fit right in there.

"If she could afford these fancy clothes and had all that cash, why didn't she just get a hotel room?" I asked. "What was she doing in my house?"

It was a rhetorical question. I wasn't really expecting an answer and I didn't get one.

Devlin held up a baggie that contained an unmarked bottle of little red pills. "I wonder what these are for."

"The lab will figure it out," Stottlemeyer said and glanced over at Monk, who was also examining some pills in a baggie, but those were sealed in a foil card with a calendar printed on it. "But I know what those pills are."

"So do I," Monk said, setting the birth control pills down and looking at me. "I was having a moment of déjà vu."

Monk and I shared a look. We'd come full circle. I glanced at Stottlemeyer and he knew it, too.

Devlin shifted her gaze between the three of us.

"What am I missing?" she asked.

"Natalie killed an intruder in this house a few years back," Stottlemeyer said. "It's how we met her."

The intruder attacked me, we struggled, and I killed him on the living room couch with a pair of scissors. The captain brought Monk in to help investigate why the guy broke into my house.

The next day Monk came back to the house, went through my stuff, stumbled upon my birth control pills, and managed to embarrass me in front of my daughter.

Monk eventually figured out what the intruder was after and solved a thorny mystery, too. When it was all over, he hired me as his assistant.

And now my house had been broken into again, there was another dead body and another package of birth control pills.

Only this time I wasn't the killer, the birth control pills weren't mine, and I wasn't a frightened single mother working as a bartender.

Now I was one of the jaded cops, a woman who'd lost track of all the corpses that she'd seen and all the murderers that she'd looked in the eye.

I was an entirely different person.

I'd known that for a little while now, but I think it wasn't until that precise moment that Monk and Stottlemeyer realized it, too.

It was a significant moment, one we absorbed in silence.

Devlin was left out of it and, judging by the look on her face, she didn't like it much. To be fair, she ended up in that position a lot when the four of us got together. I could sympathize. I'd felt that way with Monk, Stottlemeyer, and Disher for months at first.

"You've both had a long day," Stottlemeyer said. "You ought to go and let us handle this. I'll give you a call in the morning and let you know what we've turned up."

Now that he'd mentioned it, I was tired.

The idea of going to sleep sounded good to me, but it wasn't going to be in my own bed as I'd hoped, at least not tonight.

"Let me grab a change of clothes and we'll be on our way."

I made a move toward my closet but Devlin stepped in front of me.

"Sorry, I can't let you do that," Devlin said. "The whole house is a crime scene."

"It's a suicide," I said.

"We don't know what it is, or why Michelle Keeling was here, or what other evidence might be in the house," Devlin said. "Until then, you can't take anything out of here."

I looked to Stottlemeyer for support, but he sighed and shrugged his shoulders. "I'm afraid she's right, Natalie. You must have some clean clothes in your luggage you can use for a day or two."

"I didn't bring any suitcases back with me."

It took Stottlemeyer a moment, but then he got the implications and nodded to himself. "Because you weren't coming back to San Francisco to stay. You came here to pack. You've decided to keep working as cops in Summit."

Monk lowered his head with guilt. "I'm sorry, Leland."

"What are you apologizing for, Monk? I'm happy for you," Stottlemeyer said, forcing a smile. "Three of my favorite people are going to be working together doing jobs that they love. I think that's a great thing."

"Thank you, Captain," I said. "I wish it hadn't come out this way. This wasn't how we planned to tell you."

The truth was, we didn't have any plan at all.

The captain waved off my concern. "We've been friends too long to worry about that. Good news is good news."

Maybe so. But if that was true, why did Monk and I feel so lousy about it?

CHAPTER NINE:
MR. MONK CLEANS UP

I stepped outside and called a crime scene cleaning company I knew and asked them to deal with my bathroom as soon as the police released the scene.

Monk waved his hands in front of me, interrupting my call. "Wait, wait. You should tell them to do your whole house."

"But there's only blood in the bathroom," I said. "The rest of the house is uncontaminated."

"You're living in denial. Did you see those carpets?" Monk said. "How many more people have to die before you do something about it?"

I ignored Monk and finished my call with the crime scene cleaners. Thankfully, it was too dark for him to notice how dirty the exterior of my car was, or he might have suggested that I hire the crime scene cleaners to go over it, too.

When I got off the phone, he invited me

to stay the night at his apartment.

I'd been sleeping on a couch for the last few weeks so I figured one more night on one wouldn't kill me. Besides, it wasn't like I had a lot of other options. He sweetened the deal by offering me whatever I needed from his vast supply of unopened toothbrushes, toothpaste, bars of soap, and shampoos to get myself cleaned up.

So I accepted his invitation but made a slight detour on the way to his place. There was a Marshalls at the corner of Fifth and Market and I knew I could pick up a cheap change of clothes there.

I parked in the red zone, stuck my SFPD crime scene permit on the dash, and ran inside before Monk could start lecturing me about breaking the law.

I'm not a picky shopper and I'm an easy size to fit. I went straight to the clearance racks and selected a pair of jeans, some T-shirts and a blouse, underwear, and socks. In less than ten minutes, I was out the door again with my purchases and I'd made only a small dent on my credit card. I got back in the car quite pleased with myself for being so swift and thrifty.

"You forgot to buy pajamas," Monk said.

"I can sleep in my underwear," I said.

"Not on my couch you can't," he said.

"Why not?"

"Because I might want to sit on it again someday."

"You think I'm that horribly filthy and disgusting?"

"No, of course not," he said.

"I'm relieved to hear that."

"I think everybody is," he said.

"Fine. I'll sleep in my clothes."

"The clothes you wore on the plane, where you sat on a seat that thousands of other people have sat upon, sweated upon, and been airsick upon, and that you wore into your home, a palace of stained carpets and decomposing corpses?" Monk said. "Are we talking about those clothes?"

I sighed. Turned off the ignition and ran back into the store, found a tank top and a pair of sweats that could double as pajamas, and went back to the car.

"Satisfied?" I asked as I tossed the bag into the backseat.

He looked over his shoulder at the bag, then back at me. "Were they out of bathrobes?"

"And nun's habits, too," I said and drove off.

The closer we got to Monk's apartment, the more tired I became and the more alert he got, which made sense. His tranquilizers had worn off entirely and he'd gotten plenty of sleep, while I'd been wide-awake for a long and stressful day of cross-country travel, confrontations, and corpses.

I was ready for bed. But as soon as Monk opened his front door and turned on the light he gasped in horror.

"Oh my God," he said. "It's a hellhole."

I'd predicted his reaction but I hadn't planned on being around to witness it. I'd forgotten that he hadn't seen his apartment yet while he was wide-awake.

"I think you're overreacting, Mr. Monk. Your apartment is perfectly, antiseptically, freakishly clean."

"Compared to your house, of course it is. Then again, so is a public urinal," he said, taking off his jacket and hanging it up in the closet. "It's going to take us all night to clean this place, perhaps longer."

"I'm too tired to clean."

"You can't sleep in this kind of filth."

"I think I could," I said.

"This is actually a blessing. Cleaning is exactly the therapy you need right now," he said, carefully rolling up his sleeves. "You'll thank me later."

"No, I'll see you later," I said and turned back to the door.

"Where are you going?"

"I don't know, but I'll figure out something," I said and walked out.

I just didn't have the energy or patience to get into a fight with him that I was sure to lose. Even if I avoided the argument and simply refused to help him scrub, vacuum, polish, dust, and disinfect an already perfectly clean apartment, which would be rude considering I was his houseguest, he'd make so much noise doing his work that it would be impossible for me to get any rest.

So I surrendered and fled.

I got in the car and started driving toward the Bay Bridge. My initial intention was to go to Berkeley and crash with my daughter and her roommates in their apartment.

But then I decided I didn't really want to burden her with my problems, which might cause some awkwardness with her roommates. They probably wouldn't understand how a dead woman could end up in my bathtub or why I was so blasé about it.

When you work with Adrian Monk, you get used to dead bodies turning up in places you'd never expect.

I also didn't want to tell her about my new job, or that I was moving, under these circumstances.

So that left me wondering where to go next. I was considering that question when

I reached the red light at the intersection of Pine and Van Ness and the new tower of the Belmont Hotel came into view. *New* was a relative term — the original hotel was built in the early 1900s and the tower was built in the 1970s.

But seeing the hotel aroused my inner Nancy Drew. As soon as the light turned green, I pulled into the red zone across the street and took out my iPhone to surf the Web for deals at the Belmont.

I found a special weekday rate for locals that was $199 a night, but that was still pricey for me. So I called the front desk and asked them what the local rate would be for their worst room with the worst view on the worst floor, figuring it would still be better than the best room at a mediocre hotel. They offered me a room on the fourth floor located by the elevator and the ice machine and overlooking an alley for $150 a night.

That was still steep for me, but it was a terrific rate for a legendary five-star hotel in the heart of San Francisco.

So I booked the room and drove right over to the Belmont, which was on Powell Street, directly across from the cable car stop at Union Square and next door to a bakery that had been making sourdough bread since the gold rush. You couldn't get more

San Francisco than that.

I dropped off my car with the valet, who distastefully regarded my Buick as if it were one of Ellen Morse's poop products. I grabbed my bags from Marshalls, probably not a store logo they were used to seeing at the Belmont, and went inside the hotel.

The lobby was vast and ornate, with massive chandeliers, maritime-themed oil paintings, grand staircases, and a tuxedoed pianist playing tunes at a huge Steinway. You won't find that at a Motel 6.

I checked in at the front desk, rattling off a ridiculous story about my house burning down. True, it was a fabrication, but it explained my bags from Marshalls and it got me some sympathy, a coupon for a free drink, and a complimentary toiletry kit to go with my room key. I thanked the clerk and headed for the elevators, stopping for a moment to glance up at the bar, which overlooked the lobby from the second-floor terrace.

As tired as I was, I couldn't resist the idea of redeeming my coupon and doing a little detective work. It was, after all, why I was there, wasn't it?

My theory about the room was correct. It was a lot nicer than what I would have found at a three-star hotel. The décor was classy, the room was almost as clean as Monk's apartment, and the bed looked so warm and comfy that I felt myself rapidly losing my resolve to play detective.

So I tossed my bags on the bed and forced myself into the shower, where the water revived me, washing the travel and the crime scene off of my skin. I stayed under the pounding spray for what felt like hours, then dried off, brushed my teeth, and got into some of my fresh clothes from Marshalls. The ensemble wasn't Gucci or Chanel, and cost far less than one night in the Belmont's cheapest room, but I hoped nobody would notice in the dim lights of the bar.

I picked up my purse, my key, and my coupon and headed downstairs for my free drink and, I hoped, a lead or two on the dead woman in my bathtub.

The bar that I was working at when I met Monk was blue collar and unpretentious. It was a comfortable place to watch a game on TV, eat some stale pretzels, and get drunk. It catered to the lonely and the bored, the alcoholic and the desperately horny.

The Belmont's cocktail lounge was white collar and elegant. The upscale and well-dressed clientele snacked on complimentary tapas and warm almonds and spent considerably more on their libations, but they were probably every bit as lonely and bored, alcoholic and horny.

A bar is a bar, after all, no matter how much you dress up the place or the customers.

I found an empty stool, took a handful of warm almonds, and glanced around the room. Most of the women were thin, expertly and expensively styled, and showing lots of cleavage. I felt matronly by comparison. In fact, I didn't even feel like a member of the same species. I couldn't look like those women if I tried.

The women were outnumbered by the men, most of whom were in suits and, I assumed, were business travelers staying at the hotel.

The bartender cleared his throat to draw my attention. He was in his fifties, with a touch of gray in his hair and eyes that looked like they'd seen it all.

"What would you like?" he asked.

I slid my coupon over to him like it was a hundred-dollar bill. "I'd like a glass of the house white wine, please."

He nodded, took a wineglass from the shelf behind him, set it in front of me, then went off to get the bottle. He came back a moment later, filled the glass, and set the bottle aside.

In the short time it took him to get me my drink, I'd cleaned out the entire bowl of nuts. I hadn't realized how ravenous I was.

He picked up the empty bowl and, from some magic place under the counter, replaced it with one that was already full of warm nuts.

"Thanks," I said.

"Can I get you anything else?"

"Actually, yeah, maybe you can," I said and took a sip of the wine. It was wonderful. "Wow, that's really good. I'm looking for an old friend of mine, and I know this is her favorite bar, but she doesn't seem to be around tonight. Maybe you know her."

He shrugged. "What's her name, Detective?"

I was stunned but I was also very, very flattered. "I look like a cop to you?"

"The only way you'd look more like a cop is if you were wearing a uniform and a badge."

"Really?" I said, taking some more nuts. "What is it about me that's so coply?"

"It's an attitude, I suppose, a gaze that's observant, judgmental, and a bit cynical."

"I could say the same about you."

"My cynicism is different from a cop's,"

he said. "It's also your cheap clothes and the clumsy story you just told."

"So you really think I'm a cop," I said.

"Oh yeah," he said. "Most definitely."

"I could kiss you," I said. The comment surprised him and for some reason I took a lot of pleasure in that. "You're the first person who has seen that quality in me and you're a total stranger. In a silly way, it makes being a cop true for me in a way that my badge doesn't."

"Okay," he said, a little uneasy now. I guess I wasn't talking like any cop he'd ever met.

"What can you tell me about Michelle Keeling?" I had some more of my wine.

"I don't know her," he said.

"Redhead, lots of freckles, dresses like all the other women here."

"I think I know who you mean. She's in here a lot. She's classy. The guys like her."

"Any guys in particular?"

"Rich ones, usually."

"And unusually?"

"There was the guy I saw her with the last time she was in here, about two or three nights ago," he said. "He dressed almost as cheaply as you, wore a tie that went out of style during the Clinton administration, and smiled way too much, which I'd expect from someone in here who probably lives paycheck to paycheck in Walla Walla."

"Walla Walla?"

"Home of the Washington sweet onion."

"How do you know that's where he was from?" I was down to half a glass of wine and another half bowl of nuts.

"Some salesman was at the bar, writing out a label for a FedEx package, contracts he wanted to send to an onion grower in Walla Walla. He didn't know the zip code but this guy did."

"So if she usually went for rich guys, what did Michelle see in him?"

"His wallet. Warren Buffett doesn't look like a billionaire, but he is," the bartender said. "This guy didn't dress rich, but he drank Cristal like it was mineral water. So maybe he was incognito or just one of those rich guys who like to come across like a regular Joe."

"Did she leave with him?"

"She always leaves with them," the bartender said.

"Was she a hooker?"

"We don't have hookers at the Belmont," he said.

"Of course not," I said.

He frowned at me and went off to tend to another customer, leaving me with some questions to ponder. I knew more about Michelle than I did before, assuming we were both talking about the same redhead. Still, knowing she was a hooker who picked up guys at the Belmont didn't explain what she was doing in my house.

But I was too tired to do much thinking beyond that. I finished off my wine, and the almonds, and went back to my room.

CHAPTER TEN:
MR. MONK GETS A CALL

The bed was incredible. It was soft and warm with lots of fluffy pillows. I could easily have slept in until noon if my cell phone hadn't started ringing promptly at eight in the morning.

I put a pillow over my head to muffle the ringing until my voice mail snagged the call. The ringing stopped and I started to fall back to sleep. But whoever it was kept calling back every few minutes, unwilling to settle for leaving me a message, repeatedly waking me up just as I was falling off the precipice into sweet slumber.

I finally gave up and reached for the phone before I remembered that I'd left it charging on the desk across the room. That meant that I had to actually leave the bedded bliss of my linen cocoon to go get it.

Now I was pissed.

I got up, marched to the desk, and grabbed the phone, half tempted to throw it across the room, but when I saw the name on the caller ID, it took the edge off my anger.

The caller was Ambrose, Monk's agoraphobic brother, who'd only stepped out of their childhood home in Marin County maybe four or five times in the last thirty-some years. He'd left once because his house was set on fire and another time because he was poisoned, both instances related to one of Monk's murder investigations. Ambrose's most recent venture outdoors was on his last birthday. Monk and I kidnapped him and took him on a road trip in a motor home, which turned out pretty well, even though Ambrose almost got killed again by murderers. It was enough to make an average man never want to leave the house, not to mention Ambrose, but there were no hard feelings. Ambrose even bought the motor home that we'd rented, though he'd yet to venture anywhere in it.

"Hello, Ambrose," I said.

"I'm so glad I got you, Natalie. I need to see Adrian right away."

It was an emergency. I knew it because he didn't bother to say hello and he was always polite and courteous. There was also a frantic undercurrent in his voice.

"What's wrong? What's happened?"

"I'll tell you when you get here," he said. "But it's a matter of life and death."

"Then call 911," I said. "Don't wait for us."

"They can't help me. Only he can. Please hurry."

And with that, he hung up.

I sat on the edge of the bed for a moment, wondering what could be wrong, and if the situation was truly so dire, why Ambrose couldn't tell me about it over the phone.

That raised another question. If he was so eager for Monk's help, why didn't he call his brother directly instead of calling me?

And why wasn't Yuki Nakamura, his live-in assistant and girlfriend, whom he met on our road trip, there to help?

It was odd. Then again, most things involving the Monk brothers usually were.

I checked out of the Belmont, retrieved my car from the valet, and headed straight to a car wash. Whatever Ambrose's emergency might be, it would have to wait a little while longer. Monk would never get in my messy car if he saw it in the light of day.

Once the car was thoroughly cleaned, I went over to Monk's place and let myself in with my key.

Monk was going over the entry hall floor

with a Swiffer, a dust mop that picks up particles using a dry, disposable cloth. His hands were in rubber dish gloves and he was wearing an apron over his clothes.

"Good morning, Natalie. I hope you had a more restful night than I did."

I wasn't surprised that he'd had a rough night. He'd spent most of the day sleeping, thanks to the pills I gave him. His internal clock must have been completely out of whack.

"Did you get walloped by the jet lag?"

"I was thankful for it. I was up cleaning most of the night. I thought I'd never finish getting rid of all the muck," Monk said, running the mop over the shiny hardwood. "But this is the last of it."

"The apartment looks exactly the same as it did last night."

"You were in a state of shock and if that wasn't abundantly clear before, what you just said proves it and so does this." He lifted the mop, removed the cloth from the Swiffer head, and held it out to me to inspect.

"Look at that filth," he said.

It was perfectly clean. "There's nothing on it."

"It's covered with dust particles."

"They must be microscopic, because they

113

can't be seen with the naked eye."

"Why do you always have to be so lewd?" he said and carried the cloth to the garbage can in his laundry room.

I followed him. "It's an expression, Mr. Monk."

"It's a lewd expression," he said, removing his apron and hanging it on a hook on the wall.

"It means looking at something with just your eyes, unaided by any magnifying device."

"So say that," Monk said. "There's no need to use the N word."

"*Naked* is not the N word."

"It is in this house," he said. "Speaking of which, where did you sleep last night?"

"The Belmont Hotel."

"I pay you way too much," he said.

"You haven't paid me in weeks."

"It's a good thing I haven't because you obviously can't control your spending. You'd just blow right through it, living a lifestyle you can't sustain. You should be thanking me for keeping your salary safe."

"I was there one night, in the cheapest room they had, and I wanted to do some digging into the Michelle Keeling case. But I'll tell you about that later. We have more pressing concerns."

"Like your inability to hold on to money."

"Ambrose called and wants to see you right away."

"What's wrong?"

"He won't tell me," I said. "But he says it's an emergency."

"It's just a ploy to drag us out there."

"So what if it is? He doesn't leave the house and you've avoided him ever since Yuki moved in."

"Forgive me for not wanting to hang out with the Hells Angels."

"Just because she rides a motorcycle, that doesn't make her a Hells Angel."

"She has tattoos, the kind that don't wash off. And she's an ex-convict."

"None of that matters. Ambrose wants to see you and we're going out there."

"I don't see why when we could just call him back and make him tell us his problem on the phone."

Well, at least now I knew one good reason why Ambrose called me and not Monk.

"Because he's your brother, Mr. Monk. You haven't seen him in months, and it could be a long time before you see him again. Or have you forgotten why we're here?"

He looked at me for a long moment. "I did. It completely slipped my mind. How am I going to tell him that I'm moving all the way across the country?"

"I don't know," I said.

"How did you tell Julie?"

"I haven't yet," I said.

"Why not?"

"Oh, I don't know. Maybe it has something to do with walking into my house and finding a dead woman in my bathtub."

"Maybe after you tell Julie you could tell Ambrose for me."

"I can't," I said.

"You'll be on a roll," he said.

"Telling your brother that you're moving away is something you'll have to do yourself, Mr. Monk."

"Then maybe I should stay."

"You're going to give up your job as a police officer in Summit, and forfeit any future you might have with Ellen Morse, because you're afraid to tell Ambrose that you're leaving?"

"That sounds reasonable to me," he said.

I didn't feel like arguing with him. Instead, I just went to the closet, took out his coat, and handed it to him.

"Let's go," I said.

On the outside, the Monk family home in Tewksbury looked exactly as it had when the Monk brothers were growing up. It was a handsome, well-maintained Victorian on a tree-lined street with a perfectly manicured lawn. And that's how I knew something was wrong.

The last time that we were there, Yuki Nakamura's Harley-Davidson motorcycle and a class C motor home, the kind that looks like a camper-trailer eating a Ford van, were parked in the driveway.

Today, they were both gone.

From that alone, I had a pretty good idea what Ambrose's emergency was and so did Monk.

"Wipe that smile off your face," I said while we were still in my car, parked at the curb out front.

"You're the one who is always telling me to lighten up and look at the bright side."

"Not at your brother's expense," I said. "If you don't go back to being your miserable self right now, the first thing I will do when I get out of this car is pick my nose."

"You wouldn't dare."

"I'll wipe my finger on my pants and then I'll spit on the sidewalk."

"You're an animal."

"Perfect," I said, pointing at his sour face. "Hold that thought."

We got out of the car and headed up the

front walk. Ambrose was waiting for us with the front door open, but the screen door was closed.

He wore his usual ensemble — an argyle cardigan sweater vest buttoned closed over a long-sleeve flannel shirt, buttoned at the collar and cuffs, a pair of corduroy pants, and a pair of Hush Puppies identical to those worn by his brother. Instead of greeting us with his usual awkward yet endearing smile, he looked distraught.

"What took you so long?" Ambrose said, taking a big step back into the entry hall as we opened the door. "Yuki is missing and time is of the essence."

"Don't worry, Ambrose," Monk said as we came in. "We'll chase her down. How long ago did she go off with your motor home?"

"Yuki didn't take it," Ambrose said. "She moved it to the storage lot across from Beach's grocery store weeks ago because the neighbors were complaining about it."

"But how do you know it's still there?" Monk asked, closing the door.

"I don't care whether it is or not. It's Yuki that I'm worried about."

Even though Ambrose and Yuki had been living together for several months now, nothing inside the house had changed, at least not downstairs. The living room was still full of file cabinets, which contained every piece of mail that had come to the house over the last forty years, as well as tidy stacks of newspapers, magazines, and books.

"We'll bring her to justice," Monk said. "What did she take?"

"She didn't take anything. Everything of hers, except her motorcycle, is still here."

"What about everything of yours?"

"You aren't listening to me," Ambrose said. "Yuki is gone. She went to Beach's grocery store yesterday afternoon and didn't come back."

"Did you call the police?" I asked.

"Of course I did. But they were no help. They wouldn't do a thing. They never do when I call. They think I'm a crank."

"That's because you call them six or seven times a week," Monk said.

"About legitimate violations of the law," Ambrose said. "I'm a good citizen and I'm vigilant. You wouldn't believe the things I see from my window. It's a jungle out there. People would be much better off if they just stayed in their homes."

"I hate to say this, but maybe she was in an accident," I said. "Did you try calling local hospitals?"

"Of course," Ambrose said. "I'm relieved to say that she's not in any of them."

"Did you call the biker bars?" Monk asked.

"Why would I do that?" Ambrose replied.

"It's good to know you haven't completely lost your senses," Monk said. "So she's gone. It was bound to happen. All things considered, you came out of this entire sordid episode unscathed. You're better off without her."

Ambrose folded his arms across his chest and glared at his brother. "Are you better off without Trudy?"

Monk flinched. It was a low blow, bringing his dead wife into this, but he deserved it.

"It's not the same thing," Monk said. "Trudy wasn't a tattooed, ex-convict biker chick who I picked up on the road. Her skin was unblemished by ink, she was law-abiding, and she was my wife."

"Meeting Yuki is the best thing that has ever happened to me, Adrian. She's completely changed my life."

"She has? How?" Monk said. "You've been living in this house for forty years and you're still afraid to step out the door."

"But can't you see that everything else about me is different?" Ambrose said.

"You look exactly the same," Monk said. "You're even wearing the same clothes."

"Inside, Adrian. I'm a totally different person inside."

"Ipecac and an enema will have the same effect," Monk said. "Though I'd rather kill myself."

"Mr. Monk," I said, giving him a stern look, "Ambrose is trying to tell you something important."

"It's okay, Natalie," Ambrose said. "I'm used to Adrian's indifference. That's one of the reasons Yuki is so special. She lets me know every moment of every day that what I feel, and what I think, and what I do matter to her."

"Of course she did," Monk said. "You were her meal ticket."

"I love her, Adrian, and I know that she loves me."

"Then why did she leave you?" Monk said.

"Mr. Monk!" I could have slapped him. "How can you say something so cruel to your own brother?"

"Because I'm trying to knock some sense into him," Monk said. "It's called tough love."

"Adrian asked a valid question, Natalie," Ambrose said. "And here's my answer. She *wouldn't* leave me. That's why I know that

121

she's in trouble. You have to find her. I wish I could go out there and do it myself, but I can't. I'm a miserable excuse for a man. I don't deserve her."

I went over to Ambrose and gave him a hug. And for the first time ever, he didn't go rigid with discomfort, which was all the evidence I needed that Yuki had changed him. I stepped back, but kept my hands on his shoulders.

"You're a good man, Ambrose. We'll find her."

"Thank you, Natalie," he said.

"But there's something I have to know first," I said, looking him right in the eye. "What if we find her and she doesn't want to come back?"

"Then at least I'll know that she's okay," he said. "If she's happy, then I will be, too."

"That's what I wanted to hear," I said.

" 'Good riddance' is what I wanted to hear," Monk said.

"That's heartless," I said to him.

"It's better than mindless. I appear to be the only person in this room who is thinking clearly," Monk said. "Let's be honest about this, Ambrose. What do you really know about this woman?"

"Not much more than you do," Ambrose said.

What we knew was that she'd been in prison for something, that she'd killed someone, and that she'd ended up in St. Louis. An investigative journalist named Dub Clemens, who was dying of lung cancer, hired her as his assistant to help him with what he knew would be his last story. Together, they set out in a motor home, chasing clues left across the country by a serial killer. That's how we met her. And when Clemens died, Yuki came to work for Ambrose and they fell in love.

"How can you love someone you know so little about?" Monk asked.

"It's not her past that I fell in love with," Ambrose replied. "It's who she is today and who we are together."

"Do you have a photograph of her?" I asked.

He shook his head sadly. "It was a huge mistake. I just never imagined her leaving. But I'm going to take hundreds of pictures of her as soon as she gets back."

"Do you have anything that might have her fingerprints on it?"

"What for?" he asked.

"There's a possibility that Yuki Nakamura may not be her real name," I said. "If she has a criminal record, her fingerprints will give us whatever is on her in the system."

"Are you listening to what she's saying, Ambrose?" Monk asked. "Think about it. Is the woman Natalie just described someone you really want back in your life?"

Ambrose ignored him. "Good idea, Natalie. Let me see what I can find."

He went upstairs. As soon as Ambrose was out of earshot, Monk glared at me.

"Why are you encouraging him? It's obvious what happened. She couldn't stand being a prisoner in this house for another second and fled."

"You don't know that," I said.

"It's a certainty." Monk paced in front of me. "She couldn't have done this at a worse time for me. I can't tell Ambrose that I'm leaving right after she's left him. His mental health is shaky as it is."

"So that's why you're so upset. It's pure selfishness. Well, now you have a great motivation to find her, don't you?"

"Not if it's just so she can tell us that she's finished with him," Monk said.

"Then you better hope it really is true love and that she's in trouble."

"So I'm screwed no matter what happens," Monk said. "I see that my life has finally returned to normal."

Ambrose came downstairs with a book in a plastic bag. It was an owner's manual for a 386 desktop computer.

"One of my early classics," Ambrose said, handing the bag to me. "She's been reading one chapter each night before bed. It's been a revelation. I had no idea when I wrote it that I was writing erotica."

Monk did a full-body cringe. I ignored him and looked at Ambrose.

"Please don't worry," I said. "Mr. Monk won't rest, and neither will I, until we find Yuki."

"I know that you won't." Ambrose looked at Monk. "Regardless of what some of you may think of her."

CHAPTER ELEVEN: MR. MONK GOES TO THE STORE

We went from Ambrose's house to Beach's grocery store, which was where Yuki was going when she disappeared. It was located in a small shopping center a few blocks away and across the street from U-Store-It, where the motor home was supposed to be parked in storage.

As we drove by U-Store-It, I could see that the motor home was there, smack in the middle of a lot crammed with other RVs, boats, trailers, and large trucks. There were also rows of storage units with corrugated-metal roll-up doors painted bright orange.

"Someone should notify the owner of the storage facility to correct their sign," Monk said. "It was obviously written by someone who is illiterate. Even a preschooler knows how to spell *you*."

"It's shorthand," I said.

"We should leave a note, or better yet, a

correction," Monk said. "It's a blight on the entire town."

"We have other priorities," I said, and steered our car into the shopping center parking lot.

"If this was Summit, I would ticket him."

"There's no law on the books that says words on signs have to be spelled correctly."

"The law of gravity isn't on the books," Monk said. "But we are expected to follow it anyway."

"We don't have the choice."

"Exactly," he said. "It's the same thing."

I might have argued with his logic but I was distracted by a troubling sight. Yuki's motorcycle was in one of the parking spaces and her tires were slashed. I pulled in beside it and stared at those tires, which struck me as a particularly ominous sign. I could just imagine the sharp knife that was used to cut the tires and imagine what damage the same weapon could cause to a human body.

Like Yuki's.

But I was being overly and needlessly dramatic. There were no signs of blood on the motorcycle or the pavement, so I scolded myself for letting my imagination run wild.

Thinking such grim thoughts about Yuki, and only minutes into our investigation, wasn't helpful. In fact, it was damaging. I needed to objectively analyze whatever I saw without adding drama that could color my perceptions and lead us down the wrong path.

"Why are we parking here?" Monk asked. "There are other spaces that are much closer and if you park beside that Chevrolet two spaces down, the cars on this side of the aisle will be in alphabetical order."

"Because that's Yuki's motorcycle next to us," I said. "And the tires are slashed."

Monk looked over his shoulder at the next aisle. "In fact, if we could get the driver of that Acura to move his car into the first space on this side, that would be perfect."

"I need you to focus, Mr. Monk. Yuki's motorcycle being here changes things."

"I don't see how."

"Because someone slashed her tires. If it happened while she was in the store, maybe she decided to walk back home and something happened to her on the way. On the other hand, she could have abandoned her bike here for some other reason and the tires were slashed afterward, which also raises some troubling questions. What do you think?"

Monk frowned and rubbed his chin. "I think the motorcycle needs to be taken away. It doesn't belong in a row of cars. Motorcycles should have their own row."

"Forget about organizing the vehicles in the parking lot and think about Yuki. That's our mission right now."

"That's your mission," Monk said.

"He's your brother."

"Who deserves better than some motorcycle mama. She probably walked out of the store, hitched a ride with the first biker that she saw, and rode off with him to his garage, where they are happily smoking marijuana joints, taking LSD, and listening to rock music way too loud."

"When you took Ambrose on the road trip for his birthday, you did it because you wanted to open him up to the world so he could find happiness. You succeeded. It was on that trip that he met Yuki and she makes him happy, more so than he's ever been. That's the only thing about her that should matter to you."

I got out of the car and slammed the door behind me. Sometimes Monk could be so extraordinarily childish, petty, and selfish that I wondered how I could have spent so many years devoted to making his life easier. He certainly didn't try to make life easier for anyone else, not even the ones closest to him.

Perhaps it was time for me to rethink my life and my priorities.

Then again, maybe I already had.

Monk caught up to me. "When I was a kid, this store was called McCabe's. Ambrose and I used to come here and play."

I stopped outside the entrance to the store. "What did you play?"

"What every kid does. The Hunt for Expired Products," Monk said. "We'd run up and down the aisle with shopping carts, seeing who could find the most expired items in a limited amount of time and bring them to the attention of the manager."

"He must have appreciated that."

"Mr. McCabe banned us from the store," Monk said. "I resented it then, but now, with the benefit of maturity, I understand that he couldn't have kids roughhousing and engaging in shenanigans in a place of business."

"That must have been it," I said and we went inside.

He stopped and looked around. "It's hardly changed."

"You haven't been inside since you were a kid?"

"Of course not," Monk said. "I was banned."

We'd been to this same shopping center

seven years earlier, on Halloween day, when Monk was called in to investigate the shooting of an armored car driver in the parking lot. But now that I thought about it, I remembered that he had stayed in the parking lot and never went inside the store.

"I think you're safe," I said. "It's been decades and the store has changed hands since then. The ban has long since expired and been forgotten."

I turned my back on Monk and approached the customer service desk, where a portly fellow with a mini-beard on his knobby chin stood organizing coupons. He was facing a mounted microphone on an adjustable arm.

"Excuse me, are you the manager?"

"Yes, I am," he said, moving the microphone aside. "How may I help you, ma'am?"

I reached into my pocket, took out my badge, and flashed it, an action that continued to make me feel really good. "I'm Natalie Teeger. We're detectives with the Summit, New Jersey, Police Department."

"We?"

"Me and my partner." I turned to gesture at Monk, but he was gone. I looked around and saw him racing out of sight down the frozen food aisle with a shopping cart. "Who is around here somewhere."

"You're a long way from home, Detective."

"It's a big case and a vital witness might have been in your store yesterday. Her name is Yuki Nakamura. She's in her twenties, dark-haired, about —"

He interrupted me. "Yeah, I know her. She's Ambrose Monk's assistant. She was in here around four o'clock. We used to make deliveries to the Monk place two times a week until she came along. Really sweet young lady. She's saving us a bundle in time and aggravation."

"Did anything unusual happen when she was here?"

He shook his head. "Nope. She came in, got her stuff, and left."

"What about afterward?"

"Mr. Monk called about fifty times looking for her, saying she didn't come back, but like I told him, nobody knows where she went after she left the store. That guy is a strange one. He never leaves the house. Ever."

"So I've heard," I said.

"He'd pay us in exact change," the manager said. "The cash was ironed and the coins were cleaned. I swear to God."

"I believe you," I said. "Do you have any surveillance cameras on the parking lot?"

"We've got one right above the entrance to the store," he said. "It's a wide-angle view."

"Would it be possible to get the footage from yesterday afternoon?"

"I can do better than that." He opened a drawer, pulled out a business card, and wrote something on the back. "All the cameras inside and outside the store record onto a DVR. The footage goes back thirty days. You can access it online and scan through whatever you like. Here's the username and password but don't spread it around." He passed the card to me.

That's when Monk charged up with a shopping cart filled with boxed, canned, and frozen goods. He was breathing hard and there was a smile on his face. "I haven't lost my mojo."

"I'm sorry, sir, this is the customer service desk," the manager said. "You'll have to pay for your items at one of the cash registers."

"No one is buying these. They are all expired goods," Monk said. "You need to dispose of them right away."

The manager looked confused. "You came into my store just to look for expired food?"

"I feel like a kid again," Monk said to me. "Still wild at heart. It's nice to know some things never change."

The manager glanced at me. "You know this guy?"

"My partner," I said.

"You should be more vigilant about checking for expired food," Monk said. "I should never have been able to gather so many items in so little time."

"What are you?" the manager said. "The grocery police?"

I laughed and took the card off the counter before the manager could change his mind. "Thank you so much. You've been very helpful."

I started to go, but Monk held back.

"We need to make an important announcement to your customers," Monk said to the manager.

"No, we don't," I said.

But Monk was already reaching for the microphone and turning it on.

"Attention, shoppers. Would the owner of the brown Acura please move your car to the first open parking spot closest to the store? Thank you. For future reference, owners of Alfa Romeos, Audis, and Aston Martins may park in the first spot of any row if it is available. Otherwise, alphabetical order according to the make of your vehicle always applies. For instance, a Bentley or BMW may park in the next available spot, followed by a Chevrolet or Chrysler. And so forth and so on. This is true of our parking lot and any others that you may visit. Thank you for your attention and good citizenship."

He clicked the mike off. The manager stared at him suspiciously.

"Are you any relation to Ambrose Monk?" he asked.

"Of course not," I said, before Monk could answer. "Why would you think that? Thank you again for your help."

I grabbed Monk by the arm and led him quickly out of the store before he could do more damage.

"Why did you lie to the manager about me and Ambrose?" he asked once we were outside.

"I didn't want the manager to invalidate the password he gave me to view their surveillance footage or to ban you from the store forever."

"Why would he do that?"

I knew Monk would never understand how irritating it was to the management for him to gather expired products or how outrageous it was to demand that people park their cars in alphabetical order according to their brands. So I came up with an explanation he could accept.

"Because he's petty, vindictive, and small-minded. He'd want to get back at you, or worse, at Ambrose, for pointing out to him his intolerable mistakes and staggering incompetence."

"Then you did the right thing," Monk said. "Let's hope he will now, too. Between poisoning his customers with expired food and letting his parking lot devolve into anarchy, it's a wonder that store is still in business."

"I'm sure he'll remember this day as his epiphany," I said and headed for the car.

As we crossed the Golden Gate Bridge on our way back into San Francisco, I called Ambrose, told him what little we knew, and had him arrange to have Yuki's motorcycle towed back to his house for safekeeping.

The call drew a scowl from Monk, who felt that having the motorcycle at the house would "attract a bad element to the neighborhood."

"Like what?" I asked.

"Yuki Nakamura," Monk said. "And her biker friends."

"She lives there already," I said. "And if she came back, it would make things a lot easier for us. We wouldn't have to look for her anymore and you could tell Ambrose that you're leaving, and dating a woman who sells crap, without feeling guilty."

"I am not dating Ellen Morse," Monk said.

"What would you call it?"

"Altruism," Monk said. "I'm trying to save her."

"From what?"

"Disease, death, and eternal damnation. I am perhaps the only person who can get her to quit her outrageous occupation before it's too late."

"She does what she does for the same reason you do what you do," I said. "To maintain the natural balance. I was there when you told her that you understood that and that you would make an effort to accept it."

"I solve murders. That's very different from peddling poo-poo."

"Murders are violent, bloody, unpleasant, and frequently very gory. How is a mutilated, decomposing corpse any less disgusting than dung?"

"Corpses don't come from anyone's behind."

"That's it? That's what makes poop more disgusting and dangerous than murder, a crime so heinous that it merits the death penalty?"

"Not murder," Monk said. "Corpses."

"I don't follow you."

"We can't put a stop to excrement, though it's certainly something we all wish for, but we can stop murder. Excrement is a disgusting fact of life best left unseen, and properly and sanitarily disposed of, not put to use in products."

"Why not?"

"Because it's repulsive, unsanitary, and forces us to see and think about something that should be unseen and disregarded."

"But that's just it, Mr. Monk. Poop is a fact of life. Hiding from it and not thinking about it doesn't make it go away. That's why Ellen is doing what she's doing. She's trying to make us accept that excrement is natural and recognize it as a potential resource."

"And that's the insanity that I am trying to save her from," Monk said. "The same way you'd try to talk a suicidal person off the roof of a building."

"You don't see the balance that she's trying to achieve? You told her that you did. Were you lying to her?"

"No, I wasn't. I see it," Monk said and then cringed. "But I wish I didn't."

"Then why not accept it?"

"Because if she'd just change that one

thing about herself, she'd be a very exceptional woman."

"What if she said she'd be willing to stop her excrement crusade if you agreed to stop solving murders?"

"That'd be ridiculous," he said. "Why would she ever propose something like that?"

"Well, maybe she thinks if you changed that one thing about yourself, you'd be a very exceptional man. Then you could both be exceptional together."

"She's never said anything like that."

"She might," I said. "Of course, there's a way to avoid the whole issue."

"What's that?"

"You could accept each other for who you are, imperfections and all. The same way Ambrose has accepted Yuki."

That shut him up all the way to police headquarters and right up the stairs to the homicide division.

thing about herself, she'd be a very excep-

Chapter Twelve:
Mr. Monk and the Mob

When we walked into the squad room, Stottlemeyer was standing in front of Devlin's desk watching while she made notes on a file. He looked up at us as we came in.

"I was wondering when you two would amble in here," Stottlemeyer said. "I was beginning to think you'd forgotten all about the corpse in Natalie's house."

"Something came up," I said and held out the plastic bag containing the 386 computer manual. "Ambrose's girlfriend, Yuki, has disappeared. He's distraught and he's asked us to find her. So I need you to do me a favor and run the prints on this book."

Stottlemeyer looked at the bag. "Has a crime been committed?"

"The tires on her motorcycle were slashed," I said.

"And you think the slasher's prints are on that book?"

"Yuki's are," I said. "I know she spent

140

some time in prison, so I want whatever information her prints will kick back on her. It could point us in the right direction."

Monk cleared his throat. "Natalie, what the captain is trying to tell you is that your request would be an unlawful abuse of police resources. You should be ashamed of yourself for asking and imposing on your relationship with him."

Stottlemeyer snatched the bag from me. "Sure, we'll run the prints for you." He dropped the bag on Devlin's desk. "Take this down to the lab when you get a chance."

"Monk is right," Devlin said. "You're just asking me to do this to stick it to him."

"And to you, too," Stottlemeyer said. "So it's a win-win for me. On top of that, I happen to owe Natalie a lot of favors and I'd like to do something nice for Ambrose."

"Then you'll let Yuki remain unfound," Monk said. "She's a bad influence on him."

"Why's that?" Stottlemeyer asked.

"You mean besides being an ex-convict biker chick?"

"Yes," Stottlemeyer said.

"She's a wanton woman with loose morals and tattoos who fornicates all over the house," Monk said.

"Okay, Captain, I'll be glad to take the bag down to the lab," Devlin said. "I'll have them put a rush on it."

Monk looked at her with disapproval. "But I thought you agreed with me that it was a misuse of the police lab."

"That was before you criticized wanton women with loose morals and tattoos who like to fornicate all over the house," Devlin said. "I'm one of those women and we have to stick together."

Monk looked at Stottlemeyer. "Did you know this about her?"

"Nope," Stottlemeyer said.

"Doesn't it trouble you?"

"I can't say that it does," Stottlemeyer said, then turned to Devlin. "Would you share with our esteemed colleagues from the Summit Police Department what we've learned about Goldilocks?"

Devlin referred to the open file in front of her. "The ME confirms that Michelle Keeling's wounds are consistent with suicide and that she bled to death."

"I already knew that," Monk said.

"You *assumed* that," Devlin said.

"What you call assumptions," Monk said spitefully, "the rest of us call facts."

"There were no drugs and only trace amounts of alcohol in her system," Devlin continued, "so she knew exactly what she was doing when she cut her own throat with your husband's straight razor. In fact, she was very experienced when it came to cutting herself. The ME found old scars on her arms that he says were clearly self-inflicted. This was a seriously troubled woman on a downward spiral."

"What about those pills in her purse?" I asked.

"They were Rohypnol, also known as roofies, also known as the date rape drug," Stottlemeyer said. "They knock a person out and give them short-term amnesia."

Monk appeared confused. "Why would a woman have those?"

"Keeling liked to let rich guys seduce her and take her back to their rooms," Devlin said. "But before they could slip anything to her, she slipped them a few of those pills in their drinks."

I remembered when Devlin and I had done the same thing to a guy — though we were in pursuit of justice and trying to save lives — but that's another story, one Stottlemeyer knew nothing about.

"When they woke up, their memories weren't the only thing they'd be missing," Stottlemeyer said. "Their jewelry and their cash would be gone, too."

That explained where all that cash in her purse had come from, but it raised more questions than it answered, which I kept to myself for the moment to let Devlin continue with her briefing.

"Keeling has only been arrested twice, but that's probably because most of her victims were married businessmen from out of town." Devlin closed the file. "The guys didn't report the crime because they didn't want their wives to find out that they're picking up women. I'll go down to the Belmont Hotel bar tonight and see what I can find out about her."

I spoke up. "I can give you a head start. The last time Michelle Keeling was at the Belmont, which was a couple of nights ago, she picked up a guy from Walla Walla, Washington. He looked like a bumpkin but he was spreading around a lot of cash. She left with him and hasn't been back since."

Devlin looked at me with disdain. Now Monk wasn't the only one trampling her turf. "You went to the bar last night?"

I shrugged. "I had to sleep somewhere, so I figured I might as well go to the Belmont. Keeling wasn't the only woman working that bar. There were a few other regulars. You might be able to get more from those women about her than I was able to squeeze from the bartender."

Stottlemeyer smiled. "You're becoming

quite the detective."

I reached into my pocket and showed him my badge like a kid presenting a good report card to their parents. "It's my job."

Stottlemeyer looked it over as if he'd never seen anything quite like it.

"I keep forgetting that," he said and handed the badge back to me. "How did the bartender know the man was from Walla Walla?"

"The man knew the zip code," I said.

"So do I," Monk said. "And I'm not from Walla Walla. It's 99362."

"Why do you know the zip code?" Devlin asked.

"The same reason I keep up on all the area codes," Monk said. "I am a good citizen."

"I'll contact the hotel," Devlin said, "track down the guy from Walla Walla, and see what he remembers about Keeling."

"That doesn't explain what she was doing at my place," I said. "Where does she live?"

Devlin referred to the file. "Her last known address was an apartment in Potrero Hill, but that was three years ago."

"Do you think she's been squatting in empty houses since then?" I asked.

Monk shook his head. "Only your clothes were in the house. She was only there for a day, perhaps two, at the most."

"I'm sure you talked to all the neighbors," I said to Devlin and Stottlemeyer. "Did anyone notice anything unusual?"

"Nobody paid any attention to your house or even noticed you were gone," Devlin said. "They only saw the usual folks on the street — the mailman, the paperboy, the gardeners, the regular cleaning ladies and nannies."

"So much for the neighborhood watch committee," I said. "Do you have any idea how she got in my house?"

"Forensics found signs that the front lock was picked," Devlin said. "But we didn't find any lock-picking tools in Keeling's belongings or anywhere in the house."

"None of this makes any sense," I said. "The woman had five thousand dollars in her purse. She didn't have to break into empty houses for a place to sleep."

"Speaking of money," Stottlemeyer said, "we found another five thousand dollars under your mattress."

"I am paying you way too much," Monk said.

"It's not mine," I said.

"The bills were all numbered sequentially," Devlin said.

"As they should be," Monk said. "When I

get cash from the bank, I insist on that. Doesn't everyone?"

"No, they don't," Devlin said.

"More evidence that civilization is crumbling all around us," Monk said.

"And it's evidence that she got that cash from one place," Stottlemeyer said. "So I had the lab check the bills out. They were marked with tiny numbers that could only be seen under ultraviolet light. We ran those numbers through all of our law enforcement databases. So far nothing's come up."

"That's not entirely true," a voice said.

We all turned to see a guy in a jacket and tie striding in as if he owned the building. He had an expression of smug superiority on his face and a pressed shirt as stiff as the stick up his butt.

"It came up for us." He took an ID out of his pocket and held it open in front of him. "Special Agent George Cardea, FBI. We marked the money." He pocketed the badge and pulled out a folded sheet of paper, which he handed to the captain. "This is a court order, Captain, allowing me to take possession of the cash."

Stottlemeyer reviewed the order, handed it to Devlin, and faced Cardea again. "You mind telling us why the cash was marked and what Michelle Keeling was doing with it?"

"In my house," I added.

Cardea gave me a cold look. "That's what we'd like to know, Ms. Teeger. I'd advise you to tell us while there's still an opportunity for you to make a deal and cut a few years off your prison time."

"You seem to be confused," I said. "I just got back from New Jersey yesterday. I had nothing to do with any of this, whatever *this* is."

"You're denying you had anything to do with the theft," he said.

"What theft?" I asked.

"Don't play dumb, Ms. Teeger. It's unflattering to you and offensive to me."

"Hey," Stottlemeyer said, taking a step toward Cardea and invading his space. "I'm the one you should be worried about offending. I'm used to unpleasant encounters with the FBI. I accept that as part of my job. But I draw the line at you walking into my house and attempting to intimidate my people. So here's the deal. You've got one minute to explain yourself before I have you escorted out of the building with your cash shoved up your ass, assuming we can get it past your head."

But Cardea didn't seem the least bit unnerved. "I'd dial down the outrage, Captain, because when all of this comes out, you're going to want me on your side to do whatever is humanly possible to minimize the blowback on your career from your association with these two."

"These are two of the finest people I know, not to mention two of the best damn detectives I've ever worked with," Stottlemeyer said. "There's nothing you can say that would change that."

Cardea smiled as if he'd been told a mildly amusing joke. "The money you found in Natalie Teeger's home is from a half a million dollars in marked bills that undercover FBI agents, posing as representatives of Mexican drug lords, used to purchase weapons from Salvatore Lucarelli."

I felt a pang of anxiety in the pit of my stomach at the mention of Lucarelli's name. He'd been the leader of organized crime in San Francisco for decades.

Not long before I became Monk's assistant, there was a shooting in a barbershop that Lucarelli used as a front for his money-laundering operation. Lucarelli forced Monk and Sharona to help him find out who the shooter was. Monk wore a wire the whole time, trying to get incriminating information on Lucarelli for the FBI, but he failed. He did, however, catch the killer.

Then, just a few years ago, during a period when we were unemployed, a private eye hired us to clear Lucarelli, who was then in prison, in the murder of the judge assigned to preside over the mobster's trial.

And we did. We proved Lucarelli had nothing to do with the murder, which was totally unrelated to the trial.

The new judge assigned to the case ultimately sided with the defense on most of the charges against Lucarelli. He was sentenced to the time he'd already served and was released . . . and then eventually was arrested again on this new set of charges arising from the sting.

I had a bad, bad feeling about this.

"We were finally able to bring Lucarelli down," Cardea said. "And the marked cash is the key piece of evidence in our case."

"Wait a minute," Devlin said. "Lucarelli has been in jail, awaiting trial, for a year now for trying to sell weapons to Mexican drug lords. How could any of that money still be in circulation?"

"Because sometime in the last two months, all of it disappeared from the evidence room of the Federal Building," Cardea said. "We've managed to keep it quiet until now. If we don't have that money, Lucarelli walks and we're out five hundred thousand dollars."

"Four hundred ninety thousand," Monk said.

"That's right, four hundred ninety thousand," Cardea said. "For a moment, I forgot that we've just recovered ten thousand of that missing money in the home of a known Lucarelli associate."

The ache in my stomach got much worse.

"Natalie never worked for the mob," Monk said.

"No, she works for a detective who worked for the mob," Cardea said. "My thinking is, if she got ten grand for her part in all of this, you must have been paid five times that much for masterminding the theft. That's why we're searching your place for the money right now."

Monk paled. "There are strangers in my apartment?"

"As we speak," Cardea said. "Turning the place upside down and inside out."

"I hope they removed their shoes before they came in, and that they are wearing gloves, and that they don't use my restroom under any circumstances, and that they refold my clothes, and that they put everything back in the exact spot where they found it, and that they remake my bed, and that they firmly close every drawer, and that they make sure every hanger is facing the same direction, and that they straighten any crooked pictures on the wall."

"Maybe you'd like them to vacuum and dust, too," Cardea said.

"That would be great and a big relief," Monk said. "But please remind them to take the vacuum cleaner bag and dust rags with them when they leave and to clean the doorknob with a disinfectant wipe."

Devlin looked at Stottlemeyer in disbelief. "Monk and Natalie worked for Salvatore Lucarelli?"

Stottlemeyer grimaced and kind of tilted his head from side to side, a nod that was neither a yes nor a no. It didn't matter. As slim as our connection to Lucarelli was, it was still damning when combined with stolen evidence in his case turning up in my apartment beside a corpse.

"I can see how this might look bad," I said to Cardea. "Even very, very bad. But I can assure you that it's just a coincidence."

"You can assure us in an interrogation room at the Federal Building," Cardea said and gestured to the door. "Let's go."

"You're making a mistake here, Cardea," Stottlemeyer said. "Take it from me, you're going to regret it."

"If I were you, Captain, I'd start thinking about how you're going to explain to your bosses why you've employed two mob lackeys as police consultants," Cardea said, and headed out.

Monk and I walked slowly behind him as if we were headed to our executions, and I was fairly certain that we were.

CHAPTER THIRTEEN:
MR. MONK AND THE JOKE

The Federal Building at Mission and Seventh looked like an eighteen-story slab of concrete sheathed in chicken wire and glass. It was aggressively and bluntly incompatible with everything around it.

The same could be said for Special Agent Derek Thorpe, who hadn't changed much in the years since Monk and I had last seen him. Back then, the bald, black, and extremely driven FBI agent was the leader of a high-tech special unit dedicated to serial killer investigations.

At the time, Thorpe took great pleasure in degrading Monk at every opportunity and touting his own expertise. Ultimately, though, Monk solved the case himself, humiliating Thorpe so thoroughly that the unit was disbanded.

Now, apparently, Thorpe was ready for some long-awaited payback. But I'm getting ahead of myself.

Since we weren't arrested, I'd insisted on driving us to the Federal Building, though Cardea followed close behind.

After we'd gone through the X-ray, pat down, and full-body scan in the lobby, which took a slow-moving, whining, and uncooperative Monk more than an hour to complete, Cardea escorted us to a windowless interrogation room bathed in a sickly fluorescent light.

We took our wobbly seats on one side of a metal table that reminded me of the ones they used down at the morgue to perform autopsies. I didn't like the implication.

"I feel so violated," Monk said. "If they are going to pat you down, they should have an anesthesiologist on hand to put you under so you don't have to experience the ordeal. But at least they've made us comfortable in a nice room to relieve some of the tension."

I stared at him. "This is probably the bleakest, most hopeless room in the entire building."

He nodded in agreement. "They obviously brought us here as a professional courtesy. I feel more relaxed already. I think everything is going to be fine."

A few moments later, Special Agent Thorpe walked in with Cardea.

Thorpe smiled, like a vampire showing his fangs. "We meet again, Rainman."

"So that's what this is all about," I said. "You've been looking for any opportunity to make Mr. Monk feel a fraction of the humiliation you felt when he bested you and now you think you've found it."

If Thorpe could have gotten away with shooting me, he probably would have. Instead, he tried to kill me with a look as he sat down across from us. When I didn't lose control of my bladder, he opened the file in front of him as if it contained a knife he could use to finish the job.

"The facts speak for themselves, Ms. Teeger," he said, idly scratching the back of his hand. "Monk has been in bed with Salvatore Lucarelli since that barbershop massacre years ago."

"I fully cooperated with the FBI on that case," Monk said. "I wore a wire the whole time, risking my life so you could get evidence against the mob."

"But we didn't get any," Thorpe said, staring pointedly at Monk, "because you tampered with the listening device."

"It was hidden in a tie and there was a stain on it," Monk said. "All I did was wash it."

"And iron it," Thorpe said.

156

"We caught the killer," Monk said.

"But Lucarelli's mob empire continued to flourish, thanks to your sabotage. And when we finally got Lucarelli in jail, you came along again to help him out."

"Oh, give me a break," I said. "Lucarelli was arrested for racketeering, tax evasion, and extortion, not murder. It wasn't Mr. Monk clearing Lucarelli of the judge's murder that got him out of prison, it was your weak case on the other charges. You're blaming Mr. Monk for the Bureau's titanic failures. Are you suggesting we should have allowed someone else to get away with murder just so you could keep Lucarelli in prison?"

"I don't let anyone get away with anything, and that includes you, Ms. Teeger," Thorpe said. "The fact remains that you've consistently aided and abetted Lucarelli and that the stolen money from the sting that put him in jail was found in your house."

"It's a coincidence," I said.

"A big fat one," Cardea said.

"I'll grant you that," I said.

"How magnanimous of you," Thorpe said.

"But let's get real, shall we? You have extremely tight security here. There's no way anyone can come in or out of this building without passing through it," I said. "So you know that Mr. Monk and I haven't been here in over a year and that we've been in New Jersey for the last month."

"We don't think you stole the money," Thorpe said. "We believe it was done by an inside man."

"I'm so glad we've settled that," Monk said and stood up. "I knew you'd see reason."

"We think you engineered the whole thing," Thorpe said. "And then you took delivery of the money from him, skimmed off your cut, and delivered the rest of the cash to Lucarelli's people in New Jersey."

"Oh." Monk sat down again and looked at me.

"If what you say is true," I said, "how did we get all that cash through airport security?"

"We wondered the same thing," Thorpe said, scratching his hand. "So we reviewed the security footage and discovered that Monk created a major diversion, allowing you to slip the money through in the chaos."

I'd forgotten about that mess. Monk objected to being searched, which caused a scene, but then he spotted a fugitive bank robber, who bolted, causing the TSA guards to scramble after him. Thorpe was right — we probably could have snuck a polar bear through security in the midst of all that.

This was looking worse and worse for us.

Monk cleared his throat. "If I am as deviously clever as you are making me out to be, wasn't it insanely stupid of us to accept payment in marked FBI sting money and keep it in our homes?"

"You intended to launder it at some point," Cardea said, "but what you didn't expect was one of Teeger's sleazy friends to commit suicide in her house."

"Have you seen Natalie's house?" Monk said. "Of course I've been expecting it."

"I didn't know Michelle Keeling," I said. "But let's say that I did. Why didn't I get rid of the money before I called the police?"

"Shock," Cardea said.

"Jet lag," Thorpe said.

I got up. "We're leaving now."

"I didn't say you could go," Thorpe said.

"That's true, Natalie. They didn't," Monk said.

"We don't need their permission to leave, Mr. Monk. You heard what they said. Their case is a joke and I don't find it particularly funny."

"Ah, now I get it," Monk said, forcing a big smile as he got up. "It's a practical joke. The hilarity comes from the contrast between the complexity of the situation and

159

the increasing absurdity of events, until the subject of the joke finally realizes what is going on or the deception is revealed in a comical climax."

"This isn't over yet, Monk," Thorpe said. "But if you tell us who the inside man is, we might be able to cut you a deal."

Monk shook his head and followed me out. "You wacky jokesters. I thought you hated me."

"I do," Thorpe said.

Monk wagged a finger at them. "Always clowning around."

Once we were in the hall and heading back toward the stairs, I whispered to Monk, "We're in big trouble."

"I know," Monk said. "How are we going to come up with a joke on them as good as the one they pulled on us?"

"You weren't punk'd. It's no joke."

"Do you think the captain and Devlin were in on it?"

"This is serious, Mr. Monk."

"But you just said that it wasn't. You were the one who pointed out the comical incongruities."

"That doesn't mean there isn't enough circumstantial evidence to convince a jury anyway. Men have been sent to the electric chair on less. Who knows what else Thorpe and Cardea might turn up?"

He narrowed his eyes at me. "Are you punking me now?"

That's when I spotted the directory and checked out where I could find the evidence room. It was two floors below the lobby. I headed for the stairs and Monk followed along beside me. But when I kept on going, past the lobby, he gave me an odd look.

"You passed our floor," he said.

"We have one more stop to make," I said.

"Can't you hold it until you get home tonight?"

"I don't have to go to the bathroom."

"Then where are we going?"

"To the scene of the crime," I said. "Isn't that usually the first place to begin an investigation?"

We emerged from the stairwell and headed down the narrow hallway, which had an unfinished look to it, as if the contractor had run out of money for anything more extravagant than a thin coat of gray paint. Conduits and pipes ran the length of the ceiling and along some of the walls.

"What are we investigating?" Monk asked.

"The missing sting money, of course."

"It's not our problem," Monk said.

"Easy for you to say. You didn't get home from New Jersey to find a dead woman in

161

your bathtub and ten grand in marked money in your house."

"That's because I keep my house clean."

"What does cleanliness have to do with this?"

"Filth attracts a certain element," Monk said. "Why do you think rats are drawn to garbage?"

I ignored the comment, took out my badge as we approached the evidence room door, and clipped it to my belt the way Devlin wore hers. I also tried my best to imitate Devlin's aggressive posture and body language.

"Are you having cramps?" Monk asked.

"I'm getting into character. It's all about attitude. I'm trying to look like a tough cop."

"Wouldn't you look tougher without indigestion?"

"Just put on your badge and follow my lead." I took a deep breath, opened the door, and entered the room like I owned it.

It was a windowless pit that looked like an enlarged version of the interrogation room, only without its charm. The floors were scratched linoleum, the walls were cinder blocks, the lighting was fluorescent, and the temperature was cold enough to keep milk fresh without refrigeration.

The back half of the room was closed off

with thick wire-mesh screen, beyond which I could see rows of metal shelves crammed with file boxes, several padlocked cabinets of various sizes, and a walk-in freezer, which probably had something to do with why it was so cold.

There was a scuffed-up wooden desk situated directly in front of the caged area and it was covered with files and dozens of framed photos of a small white dog with big black spots and its owner, the woman who was the lone occupant of the room.

The nameplate on her desk read SPECIAL AGENT JACQUELINE NESBO. She was about my age, and in better shape, but much more pale — though that probably was an illusion created by the contrast between her skin tone and the big red pullover sweater that she was wearing. Two more sweaters were hanging from a coatrack in the corner.

"May I help you?" Nesbo asked.

"You could start by running a lint brush over your sweater," Monk said.

"Excuse me?" she said.

"I'm Detective Natalie Teeger, Summit, New Jersey, PD, and this is my partner."

"If you don't have a lint brush, I do," Monk said.

I kept talking, hoping to trample right over Monk's comment. "We're consulting with

163

the Bureau on an organized-crime case and, since we're here, I couldn't resist the opportunity to get some pointers on evidence storage and security from the expert."

"Or you could burn the sweater," Monk said. "Is there an incinerator in the building?"

She pinned Monk with a cold look. "What's wrong with my sweater?"

"It looks like it's made of dog hair," Monk said.

Nesbo plucked a hair from her sweater and flicked it aside. "Occupational hazard when you live with dogs." She looked affectionately at the photos. "But it's worth it."

"Your dog is adorable," I said, trying to salvage the situation before Monk ruined everything. "I've never seen one quite like it. What's the breed?"

"Jack Shitz," she said.

"I'm sure he does, everywhere and indiscriminately, but there's no need to tell us and no reason for profanity," Monk said. "Show some self-control, for God's sake. You're a federal agent."

Nesbo turned and gave him a long, hard look, and that was when I swiped her nameplate.

"It's a Jack Russell terrier/shih tzu mix,

also known as a Jack Shitz," she said, then turned back to me, just as I stuck the nameplate under the back of my shirt. "Was there a reason you came down here?"

"Our evidence room back in Summit is basically a storage closet. My partner here has been asked to take it over. We could use some guidance."

"He could use some manners, but I'd be glad to help." She got up, turned her back to me, and gestured to the rows of shelving beyond the grate. "Thousands of different pieces of evidence come through here every year, everything from heroin to bull semen. Each item has to be meticulously cataloged and tracked to maintain the integrity of the chain of evidence."

As she spoke in detail about the paperwork involved, I stole a small framed picture of her dog and shoved it in my purse.

"How tight is the security?" Monk asked.

"There's an agent here at all times," she said. "And nobody gets through the gate without signing the log and swiping their ID card into the reader. They also have to sign the evidence log for the particular item they are retrieving."

"What about once they are in there?" Monk said. "Are they supervised?"

"We aren't talking about unruly children,"

she said. "They get their evidence and they leave."

"What's to stop them from rummaging through evidence in other cases or removing items that they haven't signed for?"

"Personal integrity," she said. "What are you getting at?"

She had a pen on her desk with an FBI insignia on it. So I swiped it, too, and stuck it in my back pocket.

"That once they are past the gate, they are unsupervised and can do whatever they like."

"They still have to get past me," she said. "Or whoever is sitting at this desk. We're not just pencil pushers. We're crack agents ourselves."

"I never doubted it," I said, glancing at my watch. "Oh my, would you look at the time. I'd love to stay and learn more, but we have a stakeout to get to. You know how it is."

"I've been there," she said, limping out from behind her desk, "though for the last few years, I've been here. I took a bullet in the knee in 'oh-nine."

"You're filling a vital role in the justice system and we're all better off for it," I said and headed for the door. "Thanks for your help."

Monk followed me out. Once we were in the hall, he grabbed my arm. "Why did you steal all those things from the Dog Woman?"

"To prove a point." I took Nesbo's name-plate from under my shirt and shoved it into my bag.

"That you're a criminal?"

"That I'm not," I said and went up the stairs, Monk hurrying to keep up with me.

"That's not going to be easy when they catch you with Dog Woman's belongings."

"Maybe they won't."

"Then you will have succeeded in being a criminal, and then what will you have proved?"

We reached the lobby and I walked toward the exit, where another security checkpoint was set up beside two lines, one for visitors and one for employees.

Visitors were required to return their clip-on IDs to the agent who stood behind a podium, and then pass through the scanner again, as if they were about to get on a plane.

In the employee line, about half were randomly selected for screening.

"Actually, it's a win-win." I patted his back and as I removed my hand, I dropped Nesbo's pen into his lower-left jacket pocket.

"I fail to see how," he said.

"You will."

He took a step forward and immediately froze. I forgot about how sensitive he was to balance. By adding the pen to his pocket, I'd shifted the balance of his jacket.

But it was too late. I was already at the checkpoint.

I handed my pass to the agent, stepped up the conveyor belt, and put my purse on it to be x-rayed.

I walked through the scanner without setting it off and waited for my bag to come through the other side of the X-ray machine.

Monk, meanwhile, leaned to his right to compensate for the pen in his left pocket as he approached the podium. He looked like a man with hemorrhoids walking on a tightrope.

"Did you pinch a nerve or something?" the agent asked.

Monk handed over his clip-on ID. "No. What makes you say that?"

"You're walking funny," he said.

"You must be mistaken," Monk said, and tried to straighten up, but overcompensated and nearly fell over. He quickly righted himself, leaning once again to the right. Everyone was staring at him — agents, visitors, and security guards.

My bag came through the X-ray. I was

about to snatch it up when the security guard reached for it first.

"I'd like to search your bag," she said.

"Of course," I said. "Be my guest."

Monk reached the conveyor belt for the X-ray machine and faced a quandary. If he emptied his pockets and handed over the pen, he would be revealed as a thief. If he left it in his pocket and walked through the scanner, he risked having it go off and being revealed as a thief.

And Monk wasn't a risk taker.

"I confess," Monk yelled, took the pen out of his pocket, and raised his hands above his head. "Don't shoot."

The agent behind the podium took the pen from Monk's raised hand, examined it, then gave it back to him.

"It's no problem, sir. We give these away. Think of it as a souvenir."

Monk sighed with relief and lowered his hands.

That's when the security guard who was searching my bag pulled out Nesbo's name-plate and the photo of the dog.

"But these are not," she said.

The agent at the podium picked up a phone and was instantly connected to someone. "You better get down here. We have a situation in the lobby."

Monk glowered at me from the other side of the scanner. "Happy now?"

"Ecstatic," I said.

Chapter Fourteen:
Mr. Monk and
the Bad Neighborhood

Special Agents Thorpe and Cardea were called down to deal with us and when they saw the stuff that I'd taken from Nesbo's desk in the evidence room, they were not amused.

"What the hell were you trying to prove with this lame stunt?" Thorpe asked, his arms folded across his chest.

Monk folded his arms across his chest and faced me. "I'd like to know the answer to that myself."

"I've shown that your security down here is tight," I said. "We couldn't even get through with a ballpoint pen."

"We already knew that," Cardea said, folding his arms just so he wasn't left out. "We're the FBI."

"But the security in your evidence room sucks," I said. "You can walk out with anything. For all you know, whoever the thief was went in and out of there on legitimate business for weeks, taking away a stack of cash every time. It could even have been more than one person. And they could have walked it out of here without much trouble. Cash in someone's pockets isn't going to show up when someone walks through the scanner."

Thorpe looked at Monk. "Was that your plan for getting the money out?"

"I had nothing to do with the theft of the money or Agent Nesbo's personal belongings," Monk said.

"If I were you, Thorpe, I'd stop wasting your time on us and start investigating the people inside this building," I said. "You might actually accomplish something."

"We found the marked money in your home," Thorpe said. "With a corpse."

"Did it ever occur to you that maybe the money was planted in my house as a distraction?"

"No, it didn't," Thorpe said, "and this stunt doesn't change anything."

"Yes, it does," I said and waved at the cameras positioned in various corners of the ceiling in the lobby. "If you're ever dumb enough to drag us into court, it gives us some wonderful footage to show the jury to prove just how pathetic security is in the evidence room. You've given us our reasonable doubt."

I grabbed my bag and walked out.

Monk followed and joined me on the sidewalk.

"That was great," Monk said, falling into step beside me as we walked to my car.

"Really?"

"We punk'd them right back."

"*We* did?"

"And I get to keep this pen," he said and showed it to me. "It has the FBI insignia on it. How cool is that?"

"Our troubles aren't over. We still need to figure out who actually stole the money from the FBI and why Michelle Keeling had ten thousand dollars of it and why she killed herself in my house and what happened to Yuki Nakamura and do it all while we're packing up and preparing for our new lives in Summit."

"Or not," Monk said.

"What's that supposed to mean?"

"We could do nothing."

"You mean forget about the money, Michelle Keeling, Yuki, and the move to Summit?"

"Fantastic idea," he said. "I feel better already."

"You can't just ignore your problems and hope that they'll go away."

"They aren't my problems."

"They are problems for me and Ambrose."

"But, strictly speaking, not mine."

"You can't live in a sterile little bubble, unaffected by the troubles of the people you supposedly care about or the events in the world around you."

"That's my dream."

"What about the job in Summit?"

"My life would be a lot easier if I don't take it."

We reached my car. I walked around to the driver's side. "How easy is your life going to be when I'm gone, Ambrose hates you, and you're all alone?"

"We could try it and see," he said.

"Okay," I said and opened my door. "You can start by finding your own way home."

I got in the car and started the engine. Monk tried to open the passenger door, but it was locked. He pounded on the window.

"Natalie, you can't abandon me here," he said. "There are people everywhere. What if I bump into somebody? Do you really want that on your conscience?"

I waved at him. "Have a nice day."

"You're punking me, aren't you?"

I smiled at him and drove off.

My first stop was the post office, where I picked up all of my mail that had been on vacation hold. I was astonished when they handed me a large overflowing plastic box filled with magazines, bills, and promotional flyers.

I'd had no idea that I got so much stuff every month. There was probably an entire forest somewhere that was now dry, barren earth thanks to me.

I made a quick stop at my local grocery store, bought some necessities like frozen pizzas, Diet Coke, and Oreo cookies, and headed home.

I felt a sharp pang of anxiety when I saw two police cars parked at the corner, but relaxed when I realized that it wasn't my house they were at this time. The cops were at the Gossett place, a Victorian that had been under constant renovation for twenty years by its owner, a struggling singer-songwriter who played on a lot of cruise ships and was often at sea.

My house was half a block down. I pulled into my driveway and saw one of my neighbors, Mary-Ruth Denny, standing on her porch, smoking a cigarette. She was in her twenties, favored sleeveless shirts and tank tops, and always seemed to have a bra strap showing on her shoulders.

I got out of my car, opened the back door, and pulled out my big box of mail and the bag of groceries. My hands were full, so I kicked the car door closed, the loud noise catching Mary-Ruth's attention.

"Sorry about all the commotion here yesterday," I said, standing there, holding my stuff.

She nodded. "It's scary knowing that there was a murderer killing someone right next door while we were asleep in our beds."

"If it's any consolation to you, it wasn't a murder," I said. "It was a suicide."

"Was it someone you knew?"

"Nope. A complete stranger. It's pretty bizarre."

She shook her head with disgust. "This whole neighborhood is really going to hell. Yesterday someone kills herself in your house, today someone breaks into the Gossett place and trashes it. What's the world coming to?"

"There's crime everywhere, Mary-Ruth. It's just been a bad week on our block, that's all."

"No, you're wrong. This was a quiet, peaceful street when we bought this place. I don't know what happened, but now it's turning into a slum."

Obviously, her Realtor never disclosed that before Mary-Ruth and her husband moved in, I'd killed an intruder in my living room. Or that my house had been fire-bombed. Or that the previous owner of her place murdered her husband and buried him in the backyard. Compared to all that, things had been pretty quiet lately.

"I suppose you're right," I said.

"I told Frank we're moving the first chance we get," Mary-Ruth said.

"Maybe I will, too."

"Good luck with that," she said and flicked her cigarette stub onto her dry lawn. I half expected the grass to burst into flames.

"What's that supposed to mean?"

"The housing market is in the toilet as it is. But the value of our house has just plummeted even more because we're unfortunate enough to be your neighbor. Who wants to live next door to a death house? But at least we still have some value left in our home. You'll be lucky if you can give yours away."

Mary-Ruth turned to go back into her house, quite pleased with herself.

"Do you ever wonder why your rose garden is so colorful, Mary-Ruth?"

She stopped and looked back at me. "Because I use Miracle-Gro."

"No, it's because the lady who owned your house before fertilized it with her husband's putrid, decomposing corpse." The color drained from her face. "Be sure to mention the Red Roses of Death in your real estate listing."

So much for my restraint. I smiled and went to my front door. I could forget about ever borrowing a cup of sugar from Mary-Ruth.

The first thing that struck me once I got inside was how fresh it smelled and how orderly everything was. The carpets had been shampooed, the kitchen floors mopped, and everything was dusted and straightened. Even the dishes had been washed and put away.

I kicked the front door closed, dropped my box from the post office on the couch, and took my grocery bag to the kitchen, where I unloaded my stuff.

Then I took a deep breath and hesitantly walked down the hall to the bathroom. I felt an irrational sense of doom. I certainly didn't expect to see a body still in there, but even so, I couldn't shake the memory of Michelle Keeling in a tub of bloody water.

Or that she was holding my husband's razor.

But my bathroom was pristine, something it had never been before. Every surface gleamed. The glass sparkled. It was so clean, I hardly recognized it as my own. There was no sign of the bloody death that had occurred there. In fact, there was no sign that the bathroom had ever been used at all.

Where was the stained grout? The permanent water spots? The scuffed floor? Even Mitch's razor was gone, stuck in an evidence bag somewhere at police headquarters.

I stared at the shiny bathtub, wondering if I could ever use it again after what had happened in it.

Of course I could.

Why couldn't I?

How many hotel rooms had I stayed in without knowing what had happened before in the bed or the bath?

Like Mary-Ruth, who'd had no idea of her home's dark past, maybe there were things about this house I didn't know. After all, the house was at least a hundred years old. How many owners had there been? How many people had died under this roof, naturally or unnaturally?

I knew of at least one other.

I'd killed an intruder on my couch and

that hadn't stopped me from sitting there to read the Sunday paper or watch TV.

Did that make me cold and heartless?

No, it didn't.

It made me a survivor.

And at that moment I knew something else. I wanted my husband's razor back, even if a woman had slit her own throat with it.

It was mine. It meant something to me. And I wasn't going to let her take that away.

I stuck a frozen pizza in the oven, and while I waited for it to cook, I started sorting through my mail, dividing it into piles on the kitchen table. Once the pizza was ready, I brought it to the table, opened my laptop, and logged on to the Web site that the Beach's grocery store manager had given me.

I selected the security camera footage for four p.m. two days earlier and started watching.

I had a clear view of the section of parking lot directly in front of the store, the street, and the U-Store-It facility on the other side. I could even make out Ambrose's motor home.

The only activity I saw was grocery store customers coming and going.

At about 4:05, Yuki rode into the lot on

her motorcycle, pulled into a space, and took off her helmet, which she set on the seat, apparently unconcerned that it might get stolen.

She wore a leather jacket over a T-shirt, jeans, and black boots. She was in her twenties, with long black hair that fell midway down her back, where I knew she had a tattoo of a snake coiled around her spine.

Yuki strode toward the store and out of the bottom of the video frame. A moment later, a black panel van with tinted windows drove into the picture from the left and parked beside the motorcycle, completely blocking it from the view of the camera.

Nobody got out of the van. I couldn't see anyone through the tinted passenger window.

Five minutes later, Yuki walked back into the frame carrying a bag of groceries, and headed to her motorcycle, disappearing behind the van.

At first nothing happened. It might have been a still picture if not for the traffic going by on the street.

But then the van shook, and a couple of apples toppled out into the lane, followed by a splatter of milk. Then a man fell down, or at least I thought so, judging by the arm

I saw flop to the ground at the rear of the van.

Yuki ran out into view, holding her helmet in one hand, and fled across the parking lot to the street, disappearing around the corner.

What struck me wasn't the urgency of her flight, or the blood trickling from her lip, or the flash of anger — or was it fear? — that I saw in her eyes in the instant before she turned her back to the camera.

It was the blood on the helmet.

She'd hit someone with it.

Good for you, Yuki.

Another long moment passed. The van started up and the man on the ground stood. I didn't see him, I just saw his hand push against the asphalt and then his arm withdrawing from view.

But since the guy on the ground couldn't have started the van, that meant there was at least one other person involved in the fight.

The van peeled out of the parking spot and sped off after Yuki, going so fast that it fishtailed as it made the turn onto the street and around the corner.

I sat back and looked at the screen.

At the motorcycle and its slashed tires.

At the apples and the spilled milk.

And one question, out of the many swirling in my head, rose to the forefront of my mind.

Where were the rest of the groceries?

Yuki certainly didn't take them.

That meant that the men had actually picked up the bag and taken it with them.

They'd cleaned up the scene.

But why? Who were they? What did they want?

And where was Yuki now?

Chapter Fifteen:
Mr. Monk Is Left Behind

I finished off the entire pizza and watched the video a dozen more times. On each viewing, I tried to focus on a different aspect of what I was seeing, hoping to notice a telling detail that I might otherwise have missed if I kept looking only at the big picture.

The van came into the picture from the left, which meant they'd either driven in from the side entrance or they were already in the parking lot, out of camera view, when Yuki arrived.

So I backed the video up to see if I could spot when the van got there.

I could.

I saw the van pass by on the street about five minutes before Yuki showed up, but I didn't see the vehicle enter the parking lot.

That meant that they must have gone around the block and then entered the lot from the side entrance.

And then they waited.

That raised a lot of questions.

Were they waiting specifically for her?

Or was she chosen at random?

And for what?

If they were after her in particular, how did they know that she was coming?

Once she arrived, they waited for her to go inside the grocery store and then drove into the one parking space that completely blocked her motorcycle from being seen by the camera or any of the shoppers.

They also parked at an angle that prevented the camera from getting a clear shot of the van's rear license plate or the front windshield.

I didn't think that was a lucky accident. They'd planned it that way.

So they must have scouted the location in advance and knew exactly where the camera was and what it could see.

And they picked up her spilled groceries, so nothing but her motorcycle was left behind and there was no sign of a struggle.

These guys knew what they were doing.

They were professionals.

And somehow that made what I'd seen even more frightening.

I couldn't see what happened, but my assumption was that they'd slashed the tires on Yuki's motorcycle while she was shopping and when she returned, they attacked. She fought to save herself from being — what?

Robbed?

Kidnapped?

Killed?

But then things took another strange turn.

Once she was free, she didn't run into the grocery store, where she could get help and call the police.

Instead, she chose to run across the open parking lot to the street.

It made no sense.

When the van drove off after her, I froze the video and managed to get a glimpse of the license plate, but it was splattered with mud.

Another lucky accident?

Fat chance.

So did they catch her?

And if they did, what happened next? Were they holding her captive somewhere? Was her life in danger?

Or was she already dead?

I didn't even want to contemplate that. But if she got away, why hadn't she called Ambrose or the police?

What I really needed was a detective to figure this out. Supposedly, I was one (well, technically I was a cop, which was close enough), but all I had was questions and no idea where to start looking for answers, except maybe in that box of Oreo cookies. In my experience, opening a box of Oreos was always a good start for anything.

I was heading for the pantry when I heard the front door opening behind me. My heart skipped a beat and I grabbed the handiest potential weapon that I could find, the pizza slicer with the rolling blade, and whirled around to confront the intruder.

My daughter, Julie, walked in and broke into a smile when she saw me girded for battle with my deadly pizza slicer.

"Expecting trouble from Papa John?" she asked.

I dropped the slicer on the table and gave her a big hug. "It's so good to see you. What are you doing here?"

Julie took a step back, and as I looked at her, so confident and mature, her car keys in her hand, it really hit me that she wasn't a kid anymore. She was a woman.

"You may not remember this, Mom, but I grew up on this street, so when some stranger dies in our bathtub and a whole bunch of cops show up at my house, word gets back to me," she said. "What surprises me is that I heard it from my friends and not from you."

She didn't say it with anger or bitterness, more with bemusement than anything else, but still her words stung. I'd been back home for two days, and I'd been so caught up in the mysteries of Michelle Keeling and Yuki Nakamura that I forgot all about calling Julie.

"I am so sorry," I said. "I'm a terrible mother."

"No, you're not. You have a life, one I'm not as big a part of anymore, and believe me, I'm okay with that. It's something I've been looking forward to."

"You have?"

"Of course. Nobody my age wants their mom constantly looking over their shoulder. I don't even mind that much that you didn't tell me you were back in town. But you really need to call me right away when you find a dead body in our house."

"And vice versa," I said, then quickly added, "though I hope that never happens to you. Before Mr. Monk came into our lives, I would have been certain that it wouldn't, but now it wouldn't surprise me."

"Don't worry, I understood what you meant," she said. "How many times while I was growing up did I find myself involved in a murder investigation in some way? How many killers have I met? It has to be way higher than the national average for most kids."

"You have a good point. Want to share a box of Oreos with me?"

"Wow, you must really have a lot on your mind."

"I do," I said.

"Sure, let's pig out and tackle your problems," she said and we headed into the kitchen. I took the box of cookies while Julie got out a carton of milk and two glasses.

We sat down at the table and pushed aside the piles of mail, the box from the post office, the pizza carton, and my laptop.

"So, what's bugging you, Mom, besides the usual stuff with Mr. Monk?"

I opened the Oreos and she filled two glasses with milk. She liked to dip her cookies in milk but I was an Oreo purist and liked mine straight up.

"Well, there's the dead woman in our house, and the matter of some stolen federal sting money that she had with her, and there's Ambrose's girlfriend, Yuki, who is missing, or perhaps abducted, or maybe even dead, but that's not really what I need to talk to you about."

"There's more? My God, no wonder you're distracted." She dipped her cookie

189

into the milk.

I reached into my pocket and put my badge on the table between us. Julie's eyes widened in surprise.

"Who did you steal that from?"

"It's mine," I said. "Randy offered me a job as a police officer in Summit, New Jersey."

She stared at me, holding her wet cookie over her glass. "You? A cop? You're joking."

"I've actually been working as a uniformed police officer on a temporary basis for the last three weeks. And you know something?"

"Obviously I don't know anything," she said and ate her cookie.

"I liked it. And I was good at it. So I took the job."

"You did?" Julie sat back in her seat.

"Are you mad at me?"

"Surprised, that's all. It's not like it's a big stretch. You've been working with the police for years. But still, you as a cop? That's going to take some getting used to. Do you have to wear a uniform?"

"And carry a gun," I said and took a bite of my cookie.

"I can't picture it," she said.

"I'll be sure to have someone take a photo when I get back to New Jersey. Are you okay with me moving there?"

She shrugged. "It's not up to me, Mom. It's your decision."

"But what you think matters to me."

She took another cookie and pondered its complex mysteries before answering. "I think it's a big change in your life. But I also know how exciting big changes can be. I don't see why I should be the only one having all the fun."

Satisfied with herself, she dunked the cookie in her glass and took a bite.

"I'd be far away," I said.

"I love you, but some distance between us might be a good thing."

"You just got done chewing me out for not keeping in touch."

"When you find a dead body in our house," she said. "I'll miss you, but we have phones, video chat, and e-mail. And we can get together for Christmas."

"But where?" I said. "If I go to Summit, that means selling this house, or at least renting it out. We won't have a home anymore."

"I have a home. At the moment, it's an apartment in Berkeley that I'm sharing with two other girls. Yours is wherever you want it to be."

"Your father and I bought this house together. You lived here all your life. Don't you care about what happens to it?"

"I care about what makes you happy," she said. "If staying here does, then that's great. But I honestly didn't expect you to stay here forever."

"You didn't?"

"You moved around a lot before I was born, tried lots of different jobs. I figured that once I was out of the house, you'd get restless again. Apparently I was right."

"Gee, you know me better than I know myself."

"I've had twenty years to study you."

"So how come I can't figure you out? I had no idea you were this perceptive. I really thought you'd be upset about this."

"Is that why you were avoiding me?"

"Maybe, on some subconscious level," I said.

"I'm not thrilled that you're becoming a cop, and the danger that it will put you in, but at least you won't be Mr. Monk's babysitter anymore."

"Well . . ." I began. But before I could say more, there was a knock at the door. I got up to answer it.

"Don't forget this," Julie said, holding up the pizza slicer.

"Very funny," I said and went to the door.

I opened it to find Monk and Stottlemeyer standing on my porch.

CHAPTER SIXTEEN:
MR. MONK ON HIS OWN

But before I get to what brought Monk to my door, maybe I'd better go back and tell you what happened after I left him on the sidewalk outside the Federal Building (which, of course, I only found out about later from everyone involved).

He stood at the curb, waiting for me to come back. He was certain that I wasn't serious about leaving him behind and had just driven around the block to make some irrational point that only I, in my female delirium, understood.

But after ten long minutes he realized that I wasn't joking and that I'd done something truly insane.

I'd abandoned him.

For the first time in eight years, he was entirely on his own.

Even worse, he was on his own on a sidewalk crowded with people.

And their filth.

194

And their germs.

And their pets.

And the gum, dirt, garbage, excrement, spit, food, and other lethal detritus, not to mention the uneven surfaces, cracks, and paving materials that were underfoot.

A civilized person, in his view, would have taken him home before abandoning him.

Or at least left him with a cyanide pill he could take in case of an emergency, like a bird crapping on his head.

Now what was he going to do?

He'd been on his own on the streets of Summit, but that was different. This was the big city. The streets of Summit were deserted compared to those of San Francisco, where the sidewalks were teeming with mobs of perspiring, sneezing, coughing, oozing, and drooling couriers of horrific diseases and certain death.

He looked back at the Federal Building, the San Francisco home of the FBI, a law enforcement agency respected around the world.

Surely they would help him out of his plight.

How could they not?

So he took a deep breath, drew into himself so he took up as little space as possible, and plunged into the treacherous currents of foot traffic.

He kept his head down and his eyes open, deftly weaving amid the people coming and going, careful not to brush against anyone or anything as he made his way to the doors of the Federal Building.

He waited for someone to enter or leave the lobby so he wouldn't have to open the door himself. He had only a few wipes on him, so it was imperative that he ration them until he got home.

Assuming he ever made it back alive.

Monk slipped into the building as a man was leaving, barely squeezing through before the door closed. Once inside, he approached the agent who'd searched my bag.

"I require your immediate assistance," Monk said.

"What for?" she asked.

"I've been abandoned."

"What are you talking about?"

"My assistant, Natalie Teeger, just left me on the street, alone and bereft."

"Isn't that the woman who just tried to steal a bunch of stuff from the evidence room?"

"Yes, and now this. Clearly she's insane. So you can appreciate my plight. I need to get home."

"There's a bus stop on the corner," she said.

Monk shook his head. "There are people on buses."

"So call a cab," she said.

"They're even worse," Monk said. "Drunks ride in the back and vomit all over everything. People even copulate back there. Cabs are chariots of death driven by Grim Reapers with unpronounceable names."

"So call a friend. Or walk."

Monk rolled his shoulders. "What I need is for you to have an agent drive me home."

"We aren't a taxi service."

"Maybe I wasn't clear. I've been abandoned."

She stared at him. "You're a grown man."

"You are a law enforcement agency. You have a moral, ethical, and legal responsibility to make sure I get home safely."

"Maybe if you were a five-year-old kid, or someone with a serious physical handicap, or a developmentally disabled person who, without supervision, presents a grave danger to himself or others. But you don't fit any of those descriptions."

"If I am attacked by hobos or sniffed by a dog or contract a deadly disease, you will be racked with guilt every waking moment of your life," Monk said. "Are you prepared to live with that on your conscience?"

She looked him right in the eye. "Yes."

Monk glanced at the other agents and guards, who were watching this scene unfold with mild amusement.

"What about the rest of you?" Monk asked the crowd and they all nodded in agreement. "This is a disgrace. Can you at least hold the door open for me?"

"With pleasure." The woman stepped forward, held the door open, and beckoned Monk outside with an elaborate bow and sweep of her arm.

Monk put his hands in the pockets of his jacket, drew his shoulders into himself, and stepped past her.

"This is a sad, sad day for America and the future of our republic," he said.

But once he was out on the sidewalk, amid the crowd of people, he felt something in his pocket that he'd forgotten was there.

His badge.

It reminded him that he was a police officer. He was required to be courageous, to set an example for others to follow.

And he realized that he was protected by the same authority that the badge imbued him with.

He suddenly felt empowered, almost impervious to harm.

So he stood up straight, took a deep breath, and marched a few yards northeast on Mission Street, then made a sharp right on Seventh. He was determined to make the arduous journey to police headquarters, which was at the corner of Bryant, just past the Bayshore Freeway overpass.

It was less than half a mile away.

A mere three blocks. Five minutes by car and maybe fifteen minutes on foot.

And his short walk would be through the trendy, and highly gentrified, neighborhood known as SoMa, short for "South of Market" and San Francisco's would-be equivalent of New York's SoHo. The streets were lined with upscale apartments and renovated lofts, cafés and clubs, and a few car repair places and bodegas.

But he might as well have been walking barefoot across the Gobi Desert.

Everywhere he looked he saw potential peril.

And yet he persevered, thanks to the badge in his pocket and the distractions of counting parking meters and making sure he didn't step on any cracks on the sidewalk.

He was a block down the street when he saw a stray dog heading his way. It was a panting black Labrador with a jauntiness to its step that any other person would have recognized as a sign of a sunny disposition.

But Monk saw it as a symptom of rabies.

He froze in place and held his breath, so as to appear inanimate, but then feared the dog might mistake him for a tree or a fire hydrant and urinate on him.

Faced with that horrific possibility, he decided he'd rather be bitten, so he started walking slowly forward, careful not to make eye contact with the rabid beast and provoke an attack.

The dog abruptly stopped in the middle of the sidewalk, arched its back as if to sit, but then began defecating instead.

"No!" Monk yelled. "Bad dog!"

But the dog didn't listen. Monk looked around for firefighters, police officers, animal control officers, paramedics, or a clergyman — anybody who could help deal with this crisis.

There was no one, not even another passerby.

When he turned around again, there was a pile of crap on the sidewalk and the dog ambled right past him.

Faced with dog manure on the sidewalk, Monk could not go forward on either side of the street. That whole section of the block was contaminated as far as he was concerned.

So he walked back to Mission, turned to his right, walked a block west, then took Sixth Street down to Folsom, turned right, and headed back to Bryant to continue his southward journey, the dog poop a safe distance behind him. He made a mental note to call the Department of Health to send a hazardous materials team to evacuate the nearby businesses and clean the street.

Midway down the block he strolled past a Motor Moe's Automotive Center and its iconic sign featuring a cartoon depiction of a smiling, bow-tied mechanic wearing a beret and holding an oilcan in one hand and a wrench in the other. The garage's four car repair bays were open and there were three vehicles up on lifts and a Chevy Malibu on the ground, its hood open. The mechanics had stained overalls and their hands were black with oil, grease, tar, and God knew what. The shelves were in disarray and there were stains on the garage floor.

Monk tried to ignore it and move on, but he couldn't. He had a responsibility, not only as an officer of the law but as a civilized human being. He approached a mechanic working on one of the cars.

"Excuse me, sir," Monk said. "Where can I find Motor Moe? I would like to have a word with him."

The mechanic poked his head out from under the hood. He had a dab of grease on his forehead and wasn't wearing a bow tie or a beret.

"Very funny," he said. "What can I do for you, sir?"

"You could summon Motor Moe," Monk said.

"There are a hundred and fifty Motor Moe locations," he said. "If he exists, and works at one of them, it's not here. What's your problem?"

"You have three cars raised," Monk said.

"We're working on them."

"You have four cars in the garage."

"Yeah, so?"

"You need to raise your car, too," Monk said.

"But this one doesn't need to be raised for me to work on it."

"Then you need to lower one of the other cars," Monk said. "You also need to clean this place up. There's oil and grease everywhere."

"It's a garage," he said.

"And look at yourself. You're a disgrace. Motor Moe would be very disappointed in you."

The mechanic stepped up to Monk.

"What did you call me?"

"Look at Motor Moe," Monk said, pointing to the sign. "He's clean and wearing a tie and a beret. Now look at yourself. You're out of uniform and a mess."

The mechanic stared at Monk for a long moment, then nodded. "You know, you're right. We'll close up shop right away, clean up everything, and get ourselves some berets."

"And bow ties," Monk said.

"Right," the mechanic said. "Bow ties. Don't know what I was thinking, coming to work in a garage without one."

Monk smiled, missing the man's sarcasm entirely. "Your judgment was probably clouded by that beer you've been drinking."

"How do you know I drink beer?"

"There's your distinctive beer belly, for one thing," Monk said. "And you're wearing a Budweiser T-shirt. The logo is visible through the holes in your beer-stained overalls. You should burn them, by the way."

"Burn what?"

"Your overalls, your T-shirt, everything you're wearing," Monk said. "They are beyond salvation. But you aren't, nor is this establishment. You can still make Motor Moe proud."

"That's a relief," the mechanic said.

"I'm glad I stopped by," Monk said.

"Oh yeah," the mechanic said. "Me, too."

Buoyed by the positive change he'd made in the community, and in this man's life, Monk continued on his journey with renewed vigor.

But by the time he reached police headquarters and scaled the two flights of steps up to homicide, he was exhausted, parched, and desperate for water.

Stottlemeyer came out of his office just as Monk staggered in.

"What happened to you?"

"Water," Monk gasped. "Water."

The captain led him over to the kitchenette, got out a bottle of Fiji water, and handed it to him.

"Glass," Monk gasped. "Glass."

Stottlemeyer took a glass out of the dish drainer and offered it to him. But Monk wouldn't take it.

"Wash," Monk gasped. "Wash."

The captain groaned, squirted soap in the glass, and quickly rinsed it before handing it to Monk.

"Dry," Monk said. "Dry."

"If I do dry it," Stottlemeyer said, "it's going to be with my shirttail."

Monk took the glass, poured his water into it, and guzzled it down before collapsing in the nearest chair.

"Are you going to tell me what happened or not?" Stottlemeyer said. "I'm in a hurry."

"Natalie has abandoned me," Monk said.

"What do you mean?"

"She drove off and left me outside of the Federal Building. I had to get here on my own, on foot, through treacherous terrain under a scorching sun."

"What did you say or do to her that ticked her off?"

"Absolutely nothing," Monk said. "I was my usual self."

"That's actually more than enough. Sorry to hear about it. See you around."

Stottlemeyer started to go, but Monk grabbed his arm. "Wait. I need a ride home."

"I've got no one to spare," he said. "The bad guys have been busy. We're stretched real thin today."

"Okay, then you can drive me."

"That's a real honor, Monk. But believe it or not, I have more pressing responsibilities than being your personal driver. I'm on my way to a possible crime scene. Some guy in the Sunset District either burned to death or drowned or both."

"How is that possible?"

"His barbecue blew up and his burned

205

corpse was found floating in his hot tub. Devlin is already there working the case."

"You can drop me off on the way."

"Your place isn't on the way," the captain said. "It's in the opposite direction."

"Fine. I'll solve the case for you and then you can drive me home."

The captain thought about it for a moment. "You've got yourself a deal."

But first, before they could go anywhere, Monk had to call the Department of Health about the dog poop.

Stottlemeyer drove and Monk sat beside him.

Monk couldn't seem to get comfortable in his seat. He kept shifting his position, sliding to and fro, sitting up and scooting down.

The captain jammed on his brakes, the sudden stop tightening Monk's seat belt and pinning him to his seat.

"If you don't stop squirming," Stottlemeyer said, "I am going to throw you out of the car right now."

Monk looked at him. "You, too? My God, I'm being abandoned by everyone."

"Did it ever occur to you, Monk, that maybe you're the problem?"

"The seat is lumpy."

206

"I am not talking about the damn seat. I'm referring to your argument with Natalie."

"Whatever is wrong is entirely her fault."

"Because you're perfect in every way."

"Because, unlike Natalie, I behave in a consistent, predictable manner. I have routines that I follow and I conduct myself according to rules of behavior that I have defined, codified, and shared with those with whom I interact on a regular basis."

"We call them friends, Monk. Surely they have a name for them on your planet, too."

"When you familiarize yourself with another person's consistent routines, behaviors, and personal rules of conduct, and they learn and acknowledge yours, you establish an understanding, shared expectations, and clearly defined roles. That is how you maintain a balanced life and build lasting relationships."

"Really? My approach has always been to try to be an honest, dependable guy, to treat people the way that I'd like to be treated, and to accept others for who they are and not who I want them to be. I figure if I can manage that, then I won't be disappointed in myself or others as much."

Monk shook his head in disbelief. "No wonder you are on your second marriage."

"What's that supposed to mean?"

"Your way of living is irrational and inconsistent. You're constantly altering your behavior and redefining expectations to adapt to whoever or whatever is around you."

"Yeah, that sounds about right."

"That's insanity," Monk said. "How can you have any kind of stability in your life if you and everyone around you are always changing your attitudes and behavior? It's anarchy."

"I'm always going to be who I am, that's a given, and I've got some principles that I won't compromise, but otherwise I try not to be rigid in my thinking."

"Aha! Now we're getting to the root of your problem."

"I don't have a problem," Stottlemeyer said.

"You need to be rigid. A building without a solid foundation will collapse. Your foundation is composed of the rules and routines. Your foundation is consistency."

"People aren't buildings, Monk."

"They'd be better off if they were," he said. "Solid, dependable, unchanging. Look at Natalie. All of a sudden she's an entirely different person."

"It's not sudden. If you'd paid even the

slightest bit of attention to her, you'd have noticed that it has been happening for a long time now."

Monk shook his head. "She's totally changed. I don't recognize her anymore."

"Everybody changes, Monk."

"I don't."

They came to a stoplight, which gave the captain a chance to look Monk in the eye.

"Ten years ago, you were nearly put in a mental institution. You were afraid to step out of your house and when you finally did, you needed a nurse at your side," Stottlemeyer said. "Now look at yourself and tell me again that you haven't changed."

The light turned green and Stottlemeyer shifted his attention back to the street as he drove on.

"That's different," Monk said. "My wife was murdered and it took me some time to . . . to stabilize myself."

"Natalie's husband was killed. Maybe it's taken her some time to stabilize herself, too."

"It's more than that."

"It sure as hell is," Stottlemeyer said. "She met you. No one could come out of that experience unscathed. And she stuck with you for years."

"I need her," Monk said.

209

"Yeah, but maybe she doesn't need you anymore."

"Then what will I do?"

"You'll change," Stottlemeyer said.

CHAPTER SEVENTEEN:
MR. MONK AND THE BBQ

The Sunset District is a sloping plain west of Mount Sutro and south of Golden Gate Park that stretches clear down to the Pacific. Calling the place Sunset had to be someone's idea of a joke, since most of the time the whole area is blanketed with fog thick enough to make Jack the Ripper feel right at home.

Monk liked the Sunset District, and not just because the weather matched his generally gray and mopey personality.

For starters, most of the Sunset is laid out in a grid pattern and is covered with cookie-cutter, two-story, two-bedroom tract houses built by the hundreds on tiny lots from the 1920s to the 1940s.

Monk liked grids and uniformity.

On top of that, all of the north-to-south avenues were numbered and all of the west-to-east streets were given names, a pattern that Monk appreciated because it was a pattern.

The only things Monk liked as much as patterns were grids and uniformity.

The dead man's house was on a street of nearly identical homes, packed so tightly together that they were practically wall to wall, with tiny patches of grass out front that were barely larger than a welcome mat.

The house that Stottlemeyer and Monk were heading to was easy to spot, thanks to the police cars, the morgue wagon, and the fire truck parked out front.

Otherwise, it looked like all the rest of the homes on the block, except the one that was right next door. That house, while architecturally similar to the others, covered two lots.

Monk glowered at the double-sized abode as he emerged from Stottlemeyer's car.

"What's wrong?" Stottlemeyer asked. "You're looking at that house like it just spit on you."

"It breaks the pattern," Monk said. "That should never have been allowed."

"These are tiny lots, Monk, and families grow. Maybe they liked the neighborhood and didn't want to move."

Monk shook his head. "They should have respected the pattern."

"Some things are more important than

sticking to a pattern."

"Like what?"

Stottlemeyer gestured to the other house, the one surrounded by yellow crime scene tape.

"Like closing this case and getting you home. If you want that to happen, you're going to have to break your pattern of standing outside and obsessing over something that has nothing to do with why we're here."

Monk couldn't argue with that logic. They went into the house and were met at the door by Lieutenant Devlin, who grimaced when she saw that Stottlemeyer had arrived with Monk in tow.

"You didn't say you were bringing Monk with you," she said.

"I didn't know," Stottlemeyer said. "What have you got?"

"A closed case. All that's left is writing up the report. So you can wait outside, Monk."

But Monk was already peeking into the living room, which was being used as an office. It was dominated by a desk that was covered with spreadsheets, calculators, and boxes of Kleenex.

The walls were adorned with dozens of photos of a rotund, gregarious fellow at various barbecue cookouts, picnics, and festivals. He was almost always in an apron and chef's hat, standing beside a grill or a platter of barbecued meat, a big smile on his rosy-cheeked face. There were also some trophies and ribbons from barbecue competitions prominently displayed on the shelves.

But it wasn't the photos or trophies that drew Monk's immediate attention — it was the pile of wadded-up tissues spilling out of the trash can.

"What does the CDC say?" Monk asked.

"CDC?" Devlin said.

"Centers for Disease Control." Monk put a handkerchief over his nose and mouth and tipped his head toward the desk. "That desk is soaked in virulent plague."

Devlin sighed. "Terry Goodman, the dead guy who lived here, had terrible seasonal allergies. It's nothing contagious. But they killed him."

"That doesn't make sense," Monk said.

"It will," Devlin said.

"But I thought Goodman either burned to death or drowned."

"He did," she said.

Monk grimaced and rolled his shoulders, and that made Stottlemeyer smile. I would have smiled, too, if I'd been there, and for the same reason.

"Now you finally know how it feels,

Monk," the captain said.

"How what feels?" he asked.

"Being told that something that doesn't make sense does make sense and is the solution to the mystery that you haven't been bright enough to solve."

"I wasn't implying that, sir," Devlin said.

"Go ahead, indulge yourself. Get all the drama and self-satisfaction out of this that you can," Stottlemeyer said. "I mean it. Because if you've really solved this one, you deserve to have some fun."

"Okay." She led them down the hall into the kitchen as she spoke. "Goodman was single, lived alone, and worked out of his house as an accountant. He'd been suffering from sinus problems for weeks and none of the medicines that he'd been taking managed to clear his congestion."

"How do you know that?" Stottlemeyer asked.

"His pharmacist is his next-door neighbor."

"Which one?" Monk asked.

"What do you mean?"

"Which house does he live in? The big house or the little one?"

She gestured to her right, to the big house that was visible outside the window that was above the kitchen sink.

"I'd like to talk to that man," Monk said.

"There's no reason to," she said. "I already have."

"Did he tell you why he broke the pattern?"

"What pattern?" she asked.

Monk stepped up to the sink and pointed out the window. "The house is huge. Way too big for the neighborhood."

"Focus, Monk," the captain said. "We've got a violent unattended death here."

Monk noticed the row of prescription bottles lined up on the windowsill. He picked one up and read it. "Bartlett Drugs. Is Bartlett the neighbor?"

"Yes, Andy Bartlett. Why?" Devlin asked.

"Never mind," Stottlemeyer said. "Do you want to get home, Monk, or don't you?"

Monk put the bottle down. Stottlemeyer turned back to Devlin.

"Please continue."

"Goodman is a barbecue nut. He doesn't eat anything that hasn't been on a grill," she said. "So at lunchtime, he went outside to make himself a slab of baby-backs that he'd been marinating in a dry rub."

She gestured to a platter of uncooked ribs on the counter. Stottlemeyer leaned down and sniffed them.

"They smell terrific," he said. "Do you

216

think they've gone bad?"

"You want to take raw meat from a crime scene?" Monk said.

"It just seems like such a waste," Stottlemeyer said. "Did you see the guy's office? He's won awards for this. They're probably incredible."

"I also saw the thousands of tissues soaked in his mucus. Do you really think it was possible that he could lean over this meat without dripping bodily fluids on it?"

Stottlemeyer grimaced and took a step back. "You were saying, Lieutenant?"

"Goodman took the meat out of the refrigerator so that it could warm up to room temperature, then went outside to light his grill," she said and headed for the sliding glass door that opened to the backyard.

The windowpanes in the French doors had been blown out, spraying the kitchen table with shattered glass. Outside, the patio was covered with the rubble that remained from the counter that had contained the built-in barbecue, which now resembled an enormous crumpled beer can.

"Goodman opened the grill, pressed the igniter button, and the entire grill exploded, setting him aflame," Devlin said as she stepped carefully around the bits of metal, chunks of cinder block, and shards of ceramic tile on her way to the hot tub a few feet away. "He either threw himself into the Jacuzzi to put out the fire or he was blown into it. The ME hasn't determined yet whether it was the blast that killed him or if he drowned — not that it matters."

The body was gone, but the water was still discolored from the charred clothing and flesh.

Stottlemeyer frowned. "So it was a gas leak."

She nodded. "Yes, sir."

"And the poor guy didn't smell the gas because of his stuffy nose."

"A freak accident," she said.

"So his allergies did kill him. That was some mighty clever detective work, Lieutenant. Don't you think so, Monk?" The captain turned, but Monk was gone. He looked around and saw that Monk had gone back into the kitchen. "What is he up to in there?"

Devlin followed Stottlemeyer's gaze. "Being an ass. He couldn't stand that I solved a case without him, so he walked away."

She went into the house and Stottlemeyer trailed after her. They found Monk standing at the sink, picking up and examining each of the pill bottles that were lined up on the windowsill.

"What's wrong, Monk?" Devlin asked. "Feeling threatened?"

"I have ever since I walked into this house."

"Really?" she said, sharing a look with Stottlemeyer. "I have to say, I'm surprised you're man enough to admit it."

"That house next door is way too close," Monk said. "I don't know how Goodman could stand being crowded like that in his own home."

"Oh, come on," Devlin said. "We both know what this is about. And it's not that house."

"Forget it, Amy," Stottlemeyer said and turned to Monk. "Okay, let's go. We're done here. I'll take you home now."

"Isn't that Natalie's job?" Devlin asked.

"She's gone," Monk said, holding one of the pill bottles up to the light. "She abandoned me."

"You mean by becoming a cop in Summit and proving she can do more than hand you wipes," Devlin said.

"By driving off and leaving me bereft and alone in the middle of a strange city."

"You've lived in San Francisco most of your adult life," Stottlemeyer said.

"Everywhere I look, things are changing, patterns are being broken, the underpinnings of civilization are dissolving. How can I stop it?"

"You can't," Devlin said.

Monk nodded, twisted open the bottle of pills, and abruptly emptied them all into his mouth.

CHAPTER EIGHTEEN:
MR. MONK AND
THE MILESTONE

For an instant, Stottlemeyer was too stunned to move, but Devlin reacted quickly. She pushed past the captain and charged Monk, who grabbed a frying pan from the drainer to defend himself as he chewed and swallowed the pills.

"Call 911," she said to Stottlemeyer.

"What were you thinking, saying that to Monk?" the captain said. "Couldn't you see how vulnerable he is?"

"I'll handle Monk," she said.

Monk swallowed some more of the pills that were in his mouth and then said, "What do you mean by that?"

"I'm going to jam my fingers down your throat and make you vomit," she said.

"Are you insane?" Monk said, taking another swing at her. "I'd rather kill myself."

"That's not going to happen," Devlin said.

"Listen to me, Adrian." Stottlemeyer took a step toward him, hands out at his sides in a gesture of openness. "It's going to be okay, I promise you. Natalie may be gone, but I'm still here. You're not alone. You're valued. Taking your life isn't the answer."

"What makes you think I want to commit suicide?"

"You said you were bereft and alone and then you swallowed a bottle of allergy medication," Stottlemeyer said.

"That wasn't allergy medication," Monk said.

Devlin picked the bottle up off the floor. "This is prescription-strength Benadryl. It says so on the label."

"They're placebos. All of those pills are," Monk said, tipping his head toward the other bottles. "They're harmless combinations of xantham gum, cellulose, sugar, whey, lactose, cornstarch, and yeast coated with shellac to keep them from dissolving and to prevent people from tasting or smelling the ingredients."

"How do you know those pills are fakes?" Devlin asked.

"I recognized them. They are the same ones Sharona and Dr. Kroger tried to trick me with whenever they were too lazy to address my legitimate medical and psychiatric concerns."

Devlin looked back at Stottlemeyer, who

sagged with relief.

"You actually believe him?" she said incredulously. "You honestly think he can spot a placebo just by looking at it?"

"I do," Stottlemeyer said.

"It's impossible," she said.

"No, it isn't," Monk said. "There are distinct differences in shape and density between the fakes and the real drugs."

Devlin gave him a long, cold look. "Maybe I should make him puke just to be safe."

Monk took a step back and held up his frying pan, ready to strike. "What you should do is arrest Andy Bartlett."

"Who?" Stottlemeyer asked.

"The pharmacist who lives next door in the obscenely big house," Monk said.

"Not the damn house again. We can't arrest a man for adding on to his home and making it larger than the others on his street," Stottlemeyer said. "At most, it's a building code violation."

"That's a grave injustice," Monk said. "But at least there are still laws in this country against murder."

"You think Bartlett killed Goodman?" Devlin said. "Didn't you hear one word of my rundown of the case?"

"I did, and that's what proves it." Monk gestured to the pills. "These medications were prescribed by three different doctors. But what they have in common is that the prescriptions were filled at Andy Bartlett's pharmacy. Here's what happened: Bartlett wanted to expand his grotesque home even more, but his neighbors refused to sell. When Goodman began having allergy problems, Bartlett saw his chance. He filled the prescriptions with placebos, knowing that would mean that Goodman's nose would remain stuffy and he wouldn't be able to smell a thing. Bartlett also knew Goodman was a barbecue enthusiast who grilled every meal. So Bartlett sabotaged the gas and simply bided his time until . . ."

"Boom," Stottlemeyer said.

"That is the dumbest thing I've ever heard," Devlin said. "It's pure supposition without a shred of evidence."

"No, it's not," Stottlemeyer said.

"What more have we got than Monk's outrageous theory?"

The captain smiled. "We have Monk."

She looked back at Monk. "What about him?"

"He's alive and well, and if those pills were real, he'd be on the floor by now, wouldn't he?" Stottlemeyer said. "That's why he ate them, to prove his point."

Devlin was frustrated, and she was pissed,

but she couldn't deny the obvious: Monk was perfectly healthy.

"Even if he's right about the placebos, how do we know that Bartlett is the killer?" she said. "Anybody could have switched out the pills with fakes."

"Goodman lived alone," Monk said. "Bartlett was the only one who had access to all the drugs from the three different doctors and could make absolutely sure that Goodman only got placebos."

"Where's Bartlett now?" Stottlemeyer asked.

Devlin tipped her head toward the window. "Next door."

"Arrest him," Stottlemeyer said.

"And tell him that's what happens when you start breaking patterns," Monk said. "It leads to this."

Devlin gave Monk a nasty look and stormed out of the kitchen without another word.

"She's a barbarian." Monk set the frying pan in the dish drainer, took a wipe out of his pocket, and cleaned his hands. "What kind of person would even think of putting her fingers down someone's throat?"

"You should be flattered that she wanted to save your life. You've given her plenty of incentive not to."

"Like what?"

"Well, for starters, you humiliated her here today."

"She was wrong," Monk said. "Are you suggesting I should have let the pharmacist get away with murder, in addition to building a grotesquely oversized home, just to spare her feelings?"

"No, but you could have pointed out her error in a more thoughtful and collaborative manner."

"I don't see how," Monk said.

"You could have complimented her on everything that she got right and then shared with her the tiny detail that she missed, one you only caught because of specialized knowledge that she didn't have," Stottlemeyer said. "Instead, you slipped into the kitchen and swallowed a bottle of pills."

"Placebos," Monk said.

"You took a huge risk just to dramatically show her up," Stottlemeyer said. "What if you had been wrong about those pills? You'd be dead now."

"At least I wouldn't have to change."

"Too late for that," Stottlemeyer said. "You've just made a major one. I'd even go so far as to say it's life-altering."

"What do you mean?"

"Don't you realize what happened today?"

226

"Natalie abandoned me," Monk said.

"And you walked to the police station by yourself, went to a crime scene, and solved a case. That's a milestone, Monk. It's huge."

"I don't see why."

"You got to the station and did your job on your own, without an assistant. It means you're finally self-sufficient again. You can let Natalie go and not have to hire anyone else."

Monk rolled his shoulders. "And be all alone?"

"Of course not. I meant what I said before. I'll be here for you."

"Will you do my shopping?"

"I can see we're going to have to define exactly what I mean by 'here for you.'"

"Yes!" Monk cried out, startling Stottlemeyer. "My God, it's finally happened."

"What has?"

"My years of hard work and extraordinary patience have paid off. Now you know that it's necessary to list, define, and categorize your rules of conduct. This is your long-awaited breakthrough. Others may have doubted that you'd achieve it, but I never lost faith in you, Leland."

"Your faith was my guiding light, Monk," the captain said, entirely for his own amusement, since he knew that his sarcasm was completely wasted on Monk.

"When we get home," Monk said, "you can borrow some of my rules and use them as a model for your own."

"There's no need," Stottlemeyer said, heading toward the front door. "I still have the eight-volume set you gave me for Christmas."

Stottlemeyer's mistake was walking Monk to his door and, in retrospect, even he wasn't sure why he did it. If the captain had stayed in his car and just dropped Monk off, he might have made a clean getaway and I might have been spared a measure of discomfort.

But he didn't. Stottlemeyer was there when Monk opened the door to his apartment and recoiled in shock at what he saw.

"My apartment has been ransacked, pillaged, and desecrated," Monk said and ventured cautiously inside.

Stottlemeyer strode in and went right past him into the living room.

Sure, the furniture and artwork weren't precisely positioned so that everything was centered, balanced, and symmetrical, but the place was still neat and orderly.

All that was lost was the cold, sterile feeling the apartment had before, and as far as

Stottlemeyer was concerned, that was an improvement.

"You should be thankful, Monk. It looks to me like they were very careful and tried to put everything back the way they found it."

"Are you blind? It looks like a horde of rampaging, deranged Vikings rode through here on horseback. No, wait — that's too civilized to describe what has happened here."

Monk was right that it felt like people had been in his home, but not in a bad way. For the first time, the apartment actually looked lived in to Stottlemeyer, as if people had sat on the furniture, opened a drawer, or read a book from one of the shelves.

"So a chair isn't in exactly the right place, a picture isn't perfectly straight," Stottlemeyer said. "Big deal. It adds character."

"It looks like a pack of rabid wolves chased a deer through here, attacked it, ripped the corpse apart, then dragged the steaming entrails through the entire house before relieving themselves in my kitchen on the way out."

"You're overreacting, as usual. It's nothing a little straightening up can't fix." Stottlemeyer walked past Monk to the door. "And now I'll leave you to it."

"The hell you will," Monk said, joining him. "This is too big a job to tackle this late in the afternoon. There's no way that I'll be able to make this place habitable enough to sleep here tonight. It could take weeks."

"You're not staying with me," Stottle-meyer said.

Monk grimaced and came to a tough decision. "All right. Take me to Natalie's."

"I thought she abandoned you."

"She did, but even she wouldn't make me live on the street like a hobo bum."

"Aren't you the guy who called her house a pit with carpet stains that would drive a person to suicide?"

"It's a risk I'll have to take," Monk said.

"You're missing my point. You insulted her home. What makes you think that she'll welcome you inside after that?"

"Because she knows I spoke up out of a deep and abiding concern for her safety and well-being," Monk said. "Hopefully she's come to her senses by now and will show the same concern for me."

And that's how they ended up at my door.

230

CHAPTER NINETEEN:
MR. MONK GETS EVEN

When I opened my door and saw the two of them standing there, I wasn't aware yet of all of the milestones that they'd reached or the crime that they'd solved in my absence.

I'd figured that Monk would walk back to the police station to get a ride, but I didn't think he would come to see me. I could think of only one reason that they'd both shown up at my door.

"Has there been a break in one of the cases?"

"Nope," Stottlemeyer said. "But I see there's been another break-in on your block. With your police experience, you ought to start a neighborhood watch program."

"I'm not going to be here much longer," I said.

Monk shouldered past him into the house, sniffing the air. "What is that intoxicating fragrance?"

"Disinfectant," I said.

"Yes, that's it. Industrial strength," he said, and then he spun around, looking at the room in awe. "My God, it's beautiful. What did you do?"

"I didn't do anything," I said. "It was the crime scene cleaners."

"They did a spectacular job," Monk said. "It's as if they burned the house down and rebuilt it from scratch."

"It wasn't that bad," I said. Stottlemeyer stepped in and I closed the door behind him.

"I need to get them to my apartment right away," Monk said, heading down the hallway, presumably to inspect the rest of the house.

"Feel free to roam around the house," I said, knowing full well that Monk couldn't hear me and wouldn't appreciate the sarcasm if he did. "Go through the drawers and closets, too. No need to ask."

"Hey, Julie." Stottlemeyer went over to the kitchen table. "It's good to see you. How are you doing at Berkeley?"

"Real well, Captain," she said.

"You're a young woman now and you don't work for me," he said. "I think it's time you started calling me Leland."

"What do you think about Mom becoming a cop, Leland?" she asked, testing out his name to see how it rolled off her tongue. It did so clumsily.

"She's going to be a hell of a detective." He helped himself to a cookie. "She already is."

"You're just saying that so I won't object to you eating my cookies," I said. "What happened at Mr. Monk's place?"

"The FBI searched it and left a few things off-center, nothing anyone except Monk would ever notice," Stottlemeyer said. "But he did, so his suitcase is in the car."

"Suitcase?" I said.

"And a carton of Fiji water," Stottlemeyer said with a grin.

"My home is uninhabitable," Monk said, returning from his inspection of my house. "I need to stay here until the crime scene unit can renovate it."

"Why go to the trouble?" Stottlemeyer said. "You're moving to Summit anyway."

Julie looked at me. "He's going with you?"

"I haven't decided yet," Monk said.

"Randy hired him, too," I said. "If Mr. Monk goes, we'll be partners."

"Of course you will." Julie shook her head. "Are you still going to call him Mr. Monk and hand him his wipes?"

"She could refer to me by my rank, which will certainly be higher than hers, if that

233

will make her more comfortable," Monk said, then gestured to me for a wipe, snapping his fingers.

"What do you want a wipe for?" I said. "You just got done telling me the place looks spectacular."

"Except for that disgusting box from the post office that you've put on the table," he said, "where we eat."

"We?" I took the box off the table, dropped it on the floor, and swept my piles of mail into it. "Happy now?"

"I will be after I clean the table," he said. "May I?"

"Go ahead," I said.

"In answer to your earlier question, Captain, I'll never get my cleaning deposit back if I leave my apartment the way it is now," Monk said and he went to the cupboard under the sink to get my cleaning supplies, which he'd bought for me as a birthday present. "And what if I want to stay? I have a moral obligation to restore the residence to a sanitary condition."

Julie took the cookies and her milk and carried them to the coffee table in the living room. I handed my glass of milk to Stottlemeyer, picked up my laptop, and followed her.

"Is that security camera footage I see?" he

asked, looking over my shoulder as he followed me to the couch.

"It's from Beach's grocery store," I said. "The last place Yuki went before she disappeared."

"That reminds me," Stottlemeyer said. "We ran her prints and got her sheet. Yuki Nakamura isn't her real name."

"I'm not surprised," Monk said, scrubbing the table.

"Her name is Erika Ito. She was convicted of embezzlement and involuntary manslaughter in Missouri and was sentenced to eight years in state prison."

"Ambrose is a marvelous judge of character," Monk said.

"She didn't serve her full sentence," Stottlemeyer said. "The judge made some kind of procedural error in his jury instructions, so she was released on appeal after serving three years."

"Who did she embezzle and kill?" Monk asked. "A lonely bachelor living at home?"

"She hacked into Juanita Banana's accounting department and stole a million dollars from their accounts," Stottlemeyer said.

"Why did she pick a company that sells bananas?" I asked.

"Devlin and I didn't get a chance to dig

much deeper than the general facts," he said. "Maybe they just happened to have the easiest software to hack."

"Who did she kill?" Julie asked.

"An operative with Blackthorn, the security firm that Juanita Banana hired to trace their stolen money. I don't have the details, but I can get them."

"And this is the woman you want to reunite with Ambrose," Monk said to me. "For shame."

"She did her time," I said.

"She got out on a technicality," Stottlemeyer said.

I glared at him. "Now you're taking his side?"

"No, I'm entirely neutral."

"Good. Then watch this security camera footage and tell me what you think," I said and showed Stottlemeyer and Julie the video while Monk did his best to ignore us, though I saw him steal a glance or two at the screen. Afterward, I shared my analysis of the video with them.

"You've really thought this out," Julie said. "I'm impressed."

"Really?"

"Honest to God," she said. "What about you, Leland?"

He nodded in agreement. "I can't think of

anything that she missed."

"Damn," I said. "I was hoping you could, because I have nothing left to go on except a gut feeling."

"Which is?" Stottlemeyer said.

"Indigestion," Monk said, carrying the cleaning supplies back to the cupboard. "Pizza and Oreos aren't a healthy meal."

"I believe Yuki truly loves Ambrose. She knows he can't leave the house," I said. "My gut tells me she wouldn't stray far. She'd want to stay close to him."

"Is there anything you can do, Leland?" Julie asked. She was enjoying using his name.

"Nope. No crime has been committed."

"She was attacked," I said, pointing to the laptop.

"You assume that she was," Stottlemeyer said. "We didn't actually see anything. For all you know, she attacked whoever was in that van."

"You don't believe that," I said.

"No, but I have to deal in facts and with evidence, all of which are in short supply here. Not to mention the complete absence of any reason for me to be involved."

"It's a missing-person case," I said.

"Or she broke up with a guy who can't accept it," Stottlemeyer said.

"I can," Monk said, returning to the living room. "And I think we should accept it for him."

I got up and went over to Monk. "Okay, here's the deal. You can stay here on two conditions."

"Two is a good number."

"One, you help me find Yuki and two, you help me figure out why Michelle Keeling killed herself in my house and had ten thousand dollars in stolen FBI sting money on her when it happened."

"What if we compromise?" he said. "I solve the Keeling case and we let Yuki go."

"My conditions are non-negotiable. Take it or leave it."

"Fine," Monk said. "But I'm doing it under duress."

"You live your whole life under duress," I said.

Stottlemeyer got up. "I'm glad you two got that worked out."

"I didn't hear you agree to help," I said.

"Keeling is a suicide and a theft from the FBI evidence room is a federal matter. There's nothing for me to investigate. But I'll provide oodles of moral support."

Julie got up now. "Adrian can stay in my room."

"Adrian?" I said.

"I'm an adult now and technically he's not your boss anymore, so why do I have to be so formal?" She gave me a kiss and looked at the captain. "Will you walk me to my car? This has become a dangerous neighborhood."

"It will be my pleasure." Stottlemeyer and Julie walked out, leaving Monk and me alone.

"You haven't apologized," Monk said.

"Neither have you."

"Then we're even."

"You like even," I said.

"I do," he said.

"So we're good."

"I suppose we are," he said.

CHAPTER TWENTY:
MR. MONK GOES TO JAIL

I called the crime scene cleaners and sent them over to Monk's apartment. I told them to clean the place as if it were splattered everywhere with blood, brains, and fecal matter.

"I'm not sure that's strong enough," Monk said. "Tell them it's even worse than your house."

I ignored his suggestion.

That chore done, I thought about our predicament with the feds and, in the absence of any other leads, figured it was time to go see the one person who probably had all the answers.

Salvatore Lucarelli.

I didn't expect the mobster to confess, but perhaps we'd learn something that might help us. I shared my thinking with Monk and he agreed.

Because Lucarelli was awaiting trial and was remanded to custody until then, he was being housed at the jail downtown on Seventh Street. The building was an architectural showplace, all undulating curves of frosted glass, which made it look more like it was designed for shopping than for incarceration.

We were led to an interview room where Lucarelli was already waiting in his yellow prison jumpsuit, his arms and legs shackled to a chain locked into a metal loop on the floor. It seemed like overkill given that Lucarelli was in his late sixties, his body was frail, and his face resembled a drowsy basset hound more than, say, a raging pit bull.

But you don't take chances with the most powerful mobster on the West Coast, a man who reputedly sat and ate lunch while watching one of his rivals being beaten with baseball bats, then stuffed alive into an oil drum and coated with lye.

Lucarelli smiled warmly as we came in. "Mr. Monk, Ms. Teeger, what a pleasant surprise. You two visit me more often when I'm in jail than my own family."

"That's because your eldest son is in prison for attempted murder," Monk said.

"And your youngest son jumped bail on extortion charges and is on the run in South America," I said, "where he is reputedly running your drug operation."

Lucarelli waved off the comments as if they were irrelevant. "It's the thought that counts, especially since I won't be in here much longer. My lawyer tells me the case against me has crumbled."

"So we've heard," I said. "That's why we're here. We'd like to know how you did it."

"You think I arranged for the theft of the marked money from the evidence room in the Federal Building?" he said.

"You're the only one who benefits from it," Monk said.

"How about the guy who took it?" Lucarelli said. "He's five hundred thousand dollars richer."

"Or more, depending on what you paid him," I said.

"I had nothing to do with the money being taken and if I did, I certainly wouldn't admit it to you," he said. "Besides, what do you care? It has nothing to do with you."

"Exactly," I said. "That's why we don't understand why you'd drag us into this by planting some of the cash in my house."

Lucarelli leaned back in his metal chair and regarded us with amusement. "You've got the money?"

"Only ten thousand of it," Monk said. "Five thousand was under her bed, the rest was in the purse that belonged to the dead woman in Natalie's bathtub."

"Michelle Keeling," I said. "But you probably know all about her."

"I've never heard of her," Lucarelli said. "Is she the one who took the money?"

"We don't know," Monk said. "Now the FBI thinks we had something to do with the theft because Natalie works for me and I've reluctantly helped you in the past."

"Wow," Lucarelli said. "You're really jammed up."

"And we really want to thank you for that," I said.

"I feel real bad about this," Lucarelli said.

"I'm sure you do," I said.

"I've got no reason to cause you any misery. I'm genuinely grateful for all that you've done for me in the past." Lucarelli leaned close and lowered his voice. "I'd tell my people to look into this but, to be honest, it doesn't help me any if the money is found, even if the chain of evidence is now irreparably broken."

"Particularly if your people, with or without your knowledge, had it stolen," I said.

"You're beginning to irritate me, lady. I told you I had no part in this and I am not accustomed to having to repeat myself," he said, his gaze turning icy, showing me the

243

first glimpse of the monster that lurked beneath the surface. "But let's say that I did steal the money. What would I gain from bringing Mr. Monk into it? It would only point back to me and end up biting me in the ass, because he's a genius and he's going to find out who did it."

"This is true," Monk said.

It was a strong argument for Lucarelli's innocence and that pissed me off. It meant we were even further away from a solution to the mystery.

"So who do you think did it?" I asked him.

"I wouldn't want to speculate," he said. "I'm just thankful that whoever it was did it. Tell him that for me when you catch him."

Special Agents Derek Thorpe and George Cardea were waiting for us in the hall when Monk and I came out of the interview room.

"It didn't take you two long to go crying to your boss," Thorpe said, absentmindedly scratching the back of his hand. "What did you think he was going to do for you?"

"He's going to do nothing, that's what," Cardea said. "He's going to walk free while you two take his place in the slam."

"Hardly seems fair, does it?" Thorpe said to Cardea.

"I guess there's no honor among thieves,"

244

Cardea said.

I shook my head at them. "That's all you've got? You've got to work on your act, because it's falling flat."

"The best you can hope for is that Lucarelli does nothing," Cardea said.

"Because what'll happen if he decides you were sloppy and gets worried that you might talk?" Thorpe said. "How do you suppose he'd solve that problem?"

"Maybe he'll invite you over for lunch," Cardea said.

"But if he does, he'll be the only one eating," Thorpe said. "While you two are stuffed into barrels."

We walked right past them and out of the building.

On the way home, as a courtesy to Monk, I stopped by the grocery store and bought frozen waffles, maple syrup, and two droppers for filling each individual square with syrup.

I made dinner as soon as we got home. And I have to be honest with you, it was nice sitting there, having a meal with Monk. It was also bittersweet, because I knew it might be one of the last times we enjoyed each other's quiet company in such a simple, domestic moment.

We'd long since moved past a basic employer and employee relationship and, while we rarely acknowledged it openly, we both knew it. But it was ordinary, seemingly unremarkable moments like our waffle dinner, and the familiarity we had with each other, that really drove it home for me.

I'd miss having him in my life if he didn't come with me to Summit.

I felt myself getting teary-eyed, and hated myself for it, so to get my mind off of us, I brought up the Keeling mystery again.

We briefly discussed the case but neither one of us knew what step to take next in the investigation.

How did Keeling get the stolen money?

Why was she in my house?

Why did she kill herself?

Who was the man — or woman — with heartburn who'd shared my bed with her? Was it the man from Walla Walla that she met at the Belmont Hotel? If so, where was he now?

If Lucarelli didn't have the money that was taken, who did? And why? Was it merely greed?

What we needed was a break, something else to happen that could generate some fresh leads or at least give us a new perspective on what we already knew, which was very little.

Sometimes investigations played out like that. I'd been through it many times before, but that didn't make it any less frustrating, particularly since I had a personal stake in both cases.

So we gave up and I sorted through my accumulated mail again because I'd unsorted it all when I swept everything back into the box. Most of it was junk mail, the rest was bills, most of which were overdue.

Monk took my junk mail pile and organized the items into categories, then wrapped each stack with a rubber band before throwing it out. I had no idea why he did that and I didn't care. All that mattered to me was that it kept him happy, occupied, and quiet.

By nine p.m., I was exhausted and ready for bed. I was preparing to head to my room when my cell phone rang. I looked at the caller ID. The number had a New Jersey area code but otherwise I didn't recognize it.

I answered the call.

"Hello, Natalie. This is Ellen Morse."

I was surprised to hear from her and immediately glanced at Monk. "Hello, Ellen, how are you?"

"To be honest, I'm miserable. I know it's

only been two days, but I miss Adrian terribly. I am hoping he's with you, because he's not answering his phone at home."

"You're in luck. He's right here." I held the phone out to Monk, who shook his head no, ran a finger across his throat, and put his hands together as if in prayer. I continued to hold the phone out and yelled: "Mr. Monk, it's for you. It's Ellen Morse."

He glared at me, took a wipe out of his pocket, and took the phone from me with it.

"This is Adrian Monk speaking," he said, turning his back to me.

I didn't stick around to eavesdrop. I went down the hall to my room and closed the door. Suddenly I was so tired, I didn't even have the energy to brush my teeth.

I'd been looking forward to sleeping in my own bed and not even the knowledge that a stranger had been in it made the prospect any less appealing.

I took off my clothes and slipped under the sheets.

It was an old mattress, and those years of sleeping on it had molded the stuffing so it fit my body perfectly. It was like being in the arms of an old lover. It pleased me to imagine how uncomfortable the bed must have been for Michelle Keeling, especially with a stack of money underneath it.

It was like the princess and the pea, if the princess was a suicidal, predatory temptress and the pea was stolen from a marked pod.

I slept peacefully and deeply for almost twelve hours. When I awoke a little after eight a.m., Monk was already up and making us waffles again. In fact, he was pretty much how and where I'd left him.

"Good morning," I said. "Did you sleep last night?"

"Of course I did," he said. "That's why my clothes are all wrinkled."

"There isn't a wrinkle on them."

"That's because I ironed them."

"Then they aren't wrinkled anymore."

"Yes, they are," Monk said. "Under the ironing. I can feel them."

I took a chair at the table, which was already set for two with droppers of syrup, glasses of Fiji water, silverware, napkins, and disinfectant wipes. I didn't mind having waffles again after having them for dinner, and I knew Monk certainly didn't. He liked repetition and doing things in twos.

"How did things go with Ellen last night?"

Monk rolled his shoulders and set a plate with a single waffle on it in front of me. "I told her that I'm undecided about returning to Summit."

"Meaning you've decided to stay in San Francisco."

"Yes." Monk got his own plate, put a waffle on it, and sat down at the table beside me.

I could tell by the tone of his voice that this time he really meant it.

And it changed everything.

Sure, I'd thought about what it would mean if Monk stayed in San Francisco, but I realized now that I hadn't really contemplated the full impact emotionally because I certainly didn't anticipate both the sadness and the fear that I was feeling.

Julie's moving out and going to college had forced a change in our lives, one that I was, in some ways, reacting to. She'd freed me to explore options. Moving away and leaving her behind wasn't such a big deal since she'd already left me to go off to college, even if it was only across the bay.

But it felt like Monk and I were in this together. We'd both gone to Summit. We'd both been offered jobs as police officers. And we'd both accepted the offers.

Knowing that he'd be there made the decision a lot easier. It gave me a sense of security as I embarked on something scary and new. There would still be something left of my old life that I was bringing with me besides my belongings.

Sure, some important aspects of our relationship would be changing, but we'd still be together. I'd still be seeing him every day. We'd still be side by side, solving crimes.

I would still have the familiarity, the comfort, and the safety of that relationship to depend on.

Now it was hitting me that I would be losing that, too.

I would be losing Adrian Monk.

And as infuriating, demanding, and selfish as he was, I would miss him terribly.

Because I loved him.

And because the person I'd become was a reflection of our time together.

I never would have thought of becoming a cop, or had the skills for it, if not for my years with him. And that's when I realized that, as sad and scared as I was at the thought of being without him, even if we weren't together, he'd still be with me every day . . . though I could finally stop carrying around a bag full of disinfectant wipes.

The enormity of the change I was making was now painfully clear.

And yet I didn't have any second thoughts.

But I needed to know why he did, though I suppose that, on some level, I always knew he'd stay. "Why aren't you going?" I asked and took a bite of my waffle, trying hard to sound neutral and not to betray my sadness.

"It's a big change." He squeezed syrup into one of the squares with the precision and concentration of someone working with nitroglycerin. "More than I am comfortable with."

"You aren't comfortable with any change."

"So there you have it," he said. "But it's more than that. I shared my apartment here with Trudy. She picked it out. It's where we lived when we were married. I can't leave those memories behind."

My situation with my house was pretty much the same and yet I realized I no longer had reservations about going. I knew that Mitch wouldn't want me keeping the house like a shrine and I couldn't use Julie as an excuse, either. She'd given me her blessing and a kick in the butt.

And yet I still felt a stab of guilt, a sense of selfishness, for walking away from the house.

"How did Ellen take it?"

"Not well," Monk said. "There was some weeping. Definitely some sniffling."

"What about her?"

"Her, too."

"You're breaking her heart," I said. "And

your own."

"It wasn't meant to be, Natalie. She's in Summit, and that's not here. She sells poop, and that's repulsive. Those are insurmountable problems."

"Not if you love each other," I said.

"I loved Trudy," he said, as if that settled the matter.

"You don't have to ever stop loving her and nobody is asking you to. I didn't know Trudy, but I'm sure that she'd want you to go on with your life, to find someone else you can love."

"You haven't."

"Not for lack of trying," I said.

"This is ridiculous. Shameful." Monk set his fork aside. "What would my mother say?"

"Excuse me?"

"Look at her two low-life sons — me, consorting with an excrement merchant, and Ambrose, fornicating with a felon in our own childhood home! This is what happens when you change."

"You find happiness," I said.

"You're missing my point."

"No, Mr. Monk." I put my hand on his and gave it a squeeze. "You are."

He didn't take his hand away or grab for a wipe.

"You can abandon me if you want," Monk said. "I think that I will be all right."

The fact that he wasn't begging me to stay, or even asking me at all, spoke volumes about how much he'd changed and how self-sufficient he'd become. I suppose I should have been hurt on some level, but I wasn't. I was proud of him.

"I know you will be," I said. "But no matter how far away I may go, I will never abandon you."

The morning crept along slowly after that. I started paying my bills and came to the unsettling realization that I was quickly running out of money. I began to wish I had that half a million in marked money in the house somewhere. But since I didn't, I reminded Monk that he still owed me my last salary check and then I sent an e-mail to Randy, telling him to deposit my salary for the weeks that I'd worked directly into my checking account. My cell phone rang and it was a call I'd known was coming and that I was dreading. The caller ID said it was Ambrose.

I couldn't send him to voice mail in good conscience, so I answered it.

"Hello, Natalie, this is Ambrose Monk calling."

"I'm so sorry I haven't called, Ambrose.

Things have been a bit hectic," I said.

Monk heard his brother's name and suddenly found something very urgent to do in another room.

"Does that mean you've made progress locating Yuki?" Ambrose asked.

"Yes and no," I said.

"I only want to hear the yes part."

"We watched security camera footage from the grocery store and it appears that some men tried to attack her or abduct her. She ran off and they followed. I think they were professionals."

"Are you sure that was the yes part? Because it sounded to me more like the no part."

"We're looking into her past to see if we can figure out who might want to harm her," I said. "We've learned a few things about who she once was."

I told him that she'd stolen money from the Juanita Banana Company and accidentally killed an operative from Blackthorn Security that they'd hired to find her.

"How does that get us any closer to finding her?" he asked.

"I don't know," I said. "But her past is all we have to go on right now."

My cell phone started ringing again. It was Captain Stottlemeyer. It was my reprieve. I used it as an excuse to end my call with Ambrose, but not before I promised to call him back as soon as I had any new information.

I picked up Stottlemeyer's call.

"Hey, Natalie, Lieutenant Devlin has got some more information on Michelle Keeling to share with you."

"Great. What is it?"

"I'm at a homicide scene a few blocks away from you," he said. "Why don't you stop by and we'll fill you in."

It was clearly a ploy to get me to bring Monk over to do more consulting for the department, but it wasn't as if I had anything better to do, like packing up my belongings, or moving my bank accounts to the East Coast, or arranging to have my house listed for sale or immediate rental.

So, sure, why not go off to investigate a murder?

CHAPTER TWENTY-ONE:
MR. MONK GOES
TO A CRIME SCENE

I took down the address and ended the call.

Monk was all for investigating a homicide, of course. He was relieved to have something to focus his energy and attention on. With my house spotlessly clean, there was nothing for him to do but count random things, like how many spoons I had, or how many books I owned, or the number of tiles in the bathroom.

The crime scene turned out to be so close by, we would have been better off walking there, though it would have meant an uphill schlep.

It was a nice little Craftsman bungalow on a narrow street with a tiny backyard dominated by a matching Craftsman-style doghouse that we could see through the wooden slats of the fence.

The front and back yards were landscaped with gravel, drought-resistant scrub and cactus, wild lilacs and sagebrush, and a smattering of large rocks. It looked like the house was in a patch of desert. All that was missing was a few lizards sunning themselves on some bleached animal skulls.

The usual corps of uniformed cops, guys from the medical examiner's office, and forensic techs were there, but they were sitting around, waiting for Stottlemeyer to release the scene to them, and he was waiting for us.

Or, more precisely, for Monk.

The captain stood on the front porch chewing on a toothpick as we approached, Monk stepping gingerly on the gravel as if each tiny pebble were a sharp tack.

"Thanks for coming by," Stottlemeyer said.

"You said you had some information for us," I said.

"I do," Stottlemeyer said. "But does anything strike you as unusual about this crime scene?"

"We haven't seen it yet," I said.

"You were what, three minutes away?" Stottlemeyer said.

"Did we keep you waiting?"

"Maybe you haven't noticed, but the crime rate in this zip code has skyrocketed in the last couple of days. All break-ins like this. Only now someone is dead and it wasn't a suicide."

Monk shifted his weight from foot to foot. "Does this victim live here?"

"Yes. His name is Jeroen Berge. He was an architect who lived alone with his dog. He'd been away working on a retirement home project in Florida for the last week or so. His sister, who was taking care of his dog at her place while he was away, says he came home yesterday afternoon, two days earlier than he'd originally planned. She stopped by this morning to bring back his dog and found the body."

"You look like you're wearing the dog," Monk said, plucking a hair from Stottlemeyer's jacket. "A golden retriever. You might as well give the beast your jacket to mate with."

"That paints a wonderful picture," Stottlemeyer said. "Thanks a lot, Monk."

The captain turned and walked into the house. Monk hobbled after him.

"What is your problem?" I asked.

"Dogs should not be allowed to live in people's homes," Monk said. "It's unsanitary. They lose twice their body weight in hair annually and they groom themselves with their tongues."

"I meant why are you limping?"

"I've got a pebble in the treads of my left

259

shoe," he said. "It's throwing me completely off balance."

"You can feel it?"

"Jeroen Berge is dead," Monk said. "I'm not."

Berge's house had beautifully restored hardwood floors and the furniture was in the woodsy Craftsman style. Monk was undoubtedly pleased that most of the interior décor, as well as the doghouse in the back, matched the exterior design. It wasn't often he found that kind of stylistic consistency in a home. Then again, Berge was an architect, so it made sense. There was a suitcase by the door and some keys on the side table, indicating that he'd just arrived.

We found Berge's body in the main room. It was a bloodless death. He lay open-mouthed and wide-eyed on his side, a bunch of letters and magazines spilled out on the floor and furniture in front of him like large pieces of confetti.

He was Caucasian, in his thirties and casually dressed, and would have looked great if he hadn't been a corpse. His head was cocked at a gruesome and unnatural angle and his jaw was hanging oddly, too.

Lieutenant Devlin was across the room, studying a recliner that was about the size of a golf cart, its bloated cushions upholstered in the kind of plush brown velour that I thought had gone extinct with the 1975 Chrysler Cordoba. The massive chair was at odds with the Craftsman style of the place and faced a huge flat-screen TV mounted on the wall. But Monk was distracted from that inconsistency by a greater concern.

"You look like a dog," Monk said to Devlin, who immediately took offense, her entire body stiffening.

I held up my hand to stop her before things spun out of control. "Relax. He's referring to a dog hair on you."

"More like a full pelt," he said, walking around the body, hands out in front of him, framing the scene.

She noticed the hair on her jacket and began wiping it off. "It's not so bad."

"If you're going undercover as a golden retriever," Monk said.

I approached the recliner. "Is that what I think it is?" Stottlemeyer nodded. "It's an original."

"I've heard about them, and dreamed about getting one," I said, "but I've never actually seen one of these up close."

"Me, too," Devlin said.

Well, at least that was one thing we could bond over.

If a man's home is his castle, then this recliner was his throne. It was called the Captain's Chair because, as the slogan said, it put you in command of your comfort.

While Stottlemeyer, Devlin, and I admired the recliner, opulent in its garishness, Monk crouched beside the body.

"What was the medical examiner's preliminary determination on the cause of death?" he asked.

"A broken neck," Devlin said. "But I suppose now you're going to tell me that he drowned."

"I concur with Dr. Hetzer." Monk took a baggie and a pair of tweezers from his pocket and removed a piece of gravel from Berge's hair. "Berge was killed from a kick to the head that was so strong it also dislocated his jaw."

I walked around the chair, admiring it. "Would it be a horrible violation of crime scene protocol if I sat on it?"

"I hope not," Devlin said. "Because the captain and I already did."

"It's irresistible," Stottlemeyer said.

Apparently that was even true for dogs. It explained why the captain and Devlin were wearing the golden retriever.

I was starting to sit in the chair when Monk cried out.

"Don't!"

"Why not?"

"Because the dog has obviously been using it as a bed and a place to groom himself," Monk said. "You will not only pick up his hair, but his fleas, ticks, worms, and the rest of his filth."

"I'll take that chance," I said.

I sat in the chair and sank deep into the plush cushions. It was comfy and warm, embracing me like a hug. It had a built-in massage function, and like a first-class seat in an airplane, it could recline into a bed. It was the most comfortable chair I'd ever sat in.

"This is amazing," I said.

"That's nothing." Stottlemeyer opened up the hidden console on the armrest. "This baby is 3G enabled and connects to your home wireless network. You can control every electronic device in your house without moving your butt."

"Every man's dream," I said.

"All it needs is a built-in toilet and you'd never have to leave," Stottlemeyer said.

"That's truer than you think," Devlin said. "I read about a guy who weighed a hundred ninety pounds when he bought the chair and four hundred seventy pounds when firefighters had to knock out a wall and remove him from it with a crane three years later."

I patted the armrest. "So we know it's durable."

Monk stood up and began roaming around the room, tilting from side to side, not so much because of his observational technique, but because that pebble in his shoe was throwing his balance off. He kept having to grab things for support.

"You can even call the chair from your smartphone," Stottlemeyer said.

"Why would you want to do that?" Devlin asked.

"To tell the chair to set your DVR, play your phone messages, set your alarm, or chill your beer." I opened up the other armrest to reveal the built-in drink cooler. There were three cold beers already in there.

"Were there any signs of a break-in?" Monk asked.

Devlin nodded. "The intruder broke a window in a French door in back. All he had to do was reach through and unlock the door. People with French doors might as well post a sign that says, WELCOME THIEVES, RAPISTS, AND KILLERS."

I turned a dial and the chair rotated in a circle, allowing me to see the broken French door and the toppled potted cactus on the patio.

"Has anything been stolen?" I asked, mostly to show that I was paying some attention to the task at hand.

"Not that we can tell," Stottlemeyer said. "There's been a little ransacking, but we think maybe Berge walked in on the burglar just as he was getting started."

I felt bad for poor Mr. Berge, but that aside, it didn't strike me as a particularly unusual or puzzling murder, certainly not one that demanded our immediate presence.

Stottlemeyer had lured us here on the pretense of giving us information on Michelle Keeling, but it seemed to me he just wanted Monk to quickly solve a murder for him.

If that was the case, I wanted our payment up front. And in this instance, the currency was information.

"I can see this is a very complex and puzzling murder that requires the undivided attention of the greatest minds in criminal detection," I said. "But you got us here by saying you had a lead for me on Michelle Keeling."

"When did you become so hard and cynical?" Stottlemeyer asked.

"When I got my badge," I said. "So, do you have something for me or not?"

"Actually, it's Devlin who does," Stottle-meyer said.

"I went down to the Belmont bar last night and asked a few questions," she said.

"Why did you do that if Keeling's death is a suicide and the FBI is taking over the case?" I asked.

"Because Monk caught a murderer yesterday that I would have missed, so I figured that I'd do a little digging into this to pay him back," she said, glancing over at him. It was as close to a thank-you as Monk would ever get from her, but if she was expecting one in return, she was in for disappointment.

He was busy examining the mail on the floor and didn't appear to have heard what she'd said, or at least was doing a good job of pretending that he hadn't. That was okay. It meant that at least one of us in the room was still giving the Jeroen Berge murder investigation their full attention.

"The first thing I learned was that there were no guests staying at the Belmont from Walla Walla last week," Devlin said. "The guy Michelle met must have come in off the street."

"That would explain why she took him back to my place and not to his room," I said. "But not what she was doing in my house to start with."

I turned a dial on the armrest console and the lights in the room dimmed.

"The other girls say Michelle was deeply depressed," Devlin said. "She felt like she was imprisoned by her life rather than living it. She wanted to change but didn't know how to do it."

"Stealing money from the FBI evidence room wasn't the way," I said.

Devlin shook her head. "She didn't do that. If she'd been in the building, the feds would have known, the same way they knew you two weren't inside."

"What if the guy from Walla Walla was actually an FBI agent using the money he stole to party and pick up women?" I said. "She took him to my house, slipped him a mickey, and stole whatever money he had on him. That was her MO, wasn't it?"

"Yes, it was," Devlin said. "But why did she stash some of the cash under your bed?"

"You know, I think we've been looking at this the wrong way," Stottlemeyer said. "It wasn't Keeling who was staying at your house, it was the guy. He brought her back from the hotel for a little whoopee and, for whatever reason, she offed herself, so he grabbed his loot and got the hell out of there."

267

His theory made a lot of sense to me and I felt stupid for not thinking of it myself.

"So the money in her purse was what she stole from his wallet, or wherever he had it on him," I said. "The rest he hid under my bed. The cash that was found there was just bills that he accidentally left behind."

"That's what I'm saying," Stottlemeyer said. "What do you think of my theory?"

"It must have been pretty lumpy sleeping on five hundred thousand dollars." I hit another button, the chair started to hum, and a tiny joystick lit up. I pushed the joystick forward and the chair actually moved. The chair wasn't just the size of the golf cart, it drove like one, too.

"It doesn't track for me," Devlin said. "Why would an FBI agent be using Natalie's house as a love nest?"

"That's easy," Stottlemeyer said, jumping out of my way. "Because he's married and can't bring the woman home, and doesn't want to risk renting a hotel room."

"It didn't stop him from hanging out in one of the nicest bars in one of the fanciest hotels in town," Devlin said.

"And why did he pick my house?" I put the chair into reverse and nearly ran over Devlin, too.

"And how did he know she wouldn't be

there?" Devlin said.

"I didn't say it was a perfect theory," he said.

I hit another button and the shades on the windows opened. It was anticlimactic after making the chair drive, but it was still cool.

Monk stared at the window shades, rolled his shoulders, and got that serene look on his face that could mean only one of two things — he'd either dislodged the pebble from his shoe or he'd solved the case.

Stottlemeyer noticed it, too. "You already know who killed this guy?"

Monk turned and looked at me. "I know where Yuki is."

CHAPTER TWENTY-TWO:
MR. MONK AND THE GIFT

We hurried out of the house, Monk walking gingerly, as if he were stepping on hot coals. It was driving me crazy.

"Stop," I said when we got to the car. "Give me your foot."

He put his hand on the car to steady himself and lifted his left leg. I examined the bottom of his shoe and saw a pebble so small it was almost invisible to the naked eye. I flicked it out of the tread with my fingernail.

"Thank you," he said. "Wipe."

"Where is she?" I reached into my purse and held the wipe out to him.

"Not for me," he said. "For you. You've been handling the bottom of my shoes with your bare hands."

I wiped my hands. "Does Yuki have something to do with this murder?"

"No, but I know who does. Get in the car. We don't have much time. If we did, I'd wait until you could get rid of those clothes. You look like a dog walking upright."

I gave him a look. "You lied about knowing where Yuki is?"

"I know exactly where she is, but forget about her for now."

"I don't want to forget about her," I said. "I want to find her."

"I already have and we'll go see her as soon as we find him."

"Who?" I asked, rapidly losing what little patience I had left.

Monk looked back at the house and saw Stottlemeyer stepping outside, watching us.

"We're going to locate Yuki now and reunite her with my brother," Monk said to him. "Ambrose."

"Yes, I know who your brother is," Stottlemeyer said, eyeing Monk suspiciously.

"They were fornicating in my parents' house and probably will again now that I have found her."

"Good for them," Stottlemeyer said.

I got in the car just to end the conversation before it got any more awkward and cringe-inducing than it already was. Monk nodded at Stottlemeyer, then got in the car.

"Drive," Monk said.

I did. "If you don't tell me what's going on in ten seconds, I am going to throw you out of the car."

"Why do people keep threatening to do that to me?"

"You just wasted five seconds." I steered toward the first open spot along the curb.

"Okay, okay, keep going. I know who the guy was who picked up Michelle Keeling and brought her back to your house."

"Who?"

"Your mailman."

"Irwin Deeb?" I said. He was a likable, chubby guy who'd been my mailman for years. "What makes you think it's him?"

Monk took a pair of tweezers and an evidence baggie from his pocket and began plucking dog hairs from my clothes as he spoke.

"It's like the captain said — there have been an inordinate number of burglaries in your zip code, all in homes that were empty because the owners were on trips. The mailman knew how long they'd be gone because they all filed vacation holds with the post office, just like you did," Monk said, putting dog hairs into the baggie. "And, if you'll recall, the neighbors told the police they didn't see any strangers or suspicious individuals around, just the usual people."

"Like the mailman and the gardeners," I said. "Everybody saw him."

272

"They just didn't register anything suspicious about it, because he was a fixture in the neighborhood. He was probably careful about when he came and went, and if someone did see him at an unusual time, they probably figured he was making a special delivery."

"It all makes sense," I said, especially since I didn't have the most observant neighbors, which is ordinarily a plus as far as privacy is concerned. "Now we know why the guy at the Belmont bar knew the zip code for Walla Walla."

"That's no clue. Any literate person knows the nation's zip codes."

I rolled my eyes. "So what made it all come together for you?"

"Jeroen Berge coming home early from his vacation and carrying his mail. A yellow vacation hold card was among the parcels."

"I didn't see that," I said.

"You were busy playing with the dog's chair," he said, examining a black hair before putting it in the baggie.

"It wasn't the dog's chair," I said.

"So it was upholstered in dog fur."

"Never mind about the chair," I said. "Tell me how being in Berge's house led you to Yuki."

"You raised the window shades," Monk said.

"But it's not like she was standing outside the window when the shades went up. What do window shades have to do with anything?"

"You were right when you said that Yuki wouldn't wander far from Ambrose," Monk said. "The surveillance video from Beach's grocery store showed the storage lot where Ambrose's motor home is parked."

"So? The RV is still there."

"Yes, but in the video you can clearly see that the shades are up above the kitchen window of the motor home. But when we drove by the day after she disappeared, the shades were closed."

"Are you sure about that?"

He gave me a look. "Trust me, she's hiding in the motor home and she's not going anywhere."

So when Stottlemeyer asked Monk if he'd solved the Berge homicide, and Monk answered that he'd found Yuki, Monk wasn't lying. He simply wasn't telling all that he knew, which is a good thing, because he was a lousy liar. But that didn't explain why he'd withheld information from the captain.

Monk regarded his baggie, which was now full of dog hair, then my clothes. "We're going to need a Hefty bag. Or an incinerator."

"Why didn't you tell the captain about the mailman?"

"Because you need to solve this mystery."

"Too late," I said. "You just did."

"Yes, but it's your name that needs to be cleared in all of this," Monk said.

"Your name, too, Mr. Monk."

"My name is fine and well established. However, solving a high-profile case like this will burnish your reputation as a cop and start your career off in a big way. Think of it as a going-away present."

It was a surprisingly thoughtful gesture for him, and one not without considerable risk for us both if we kept what we knew from the captain. It was a risk Monk was willing to take, and he was born risk averse, so the least I could do was go along with him.

"So the mailman is on the run, hiding out in empty homes along his route," I said. "We need to get a list of people who filed vacation mail holds."

"How do we get it?"

"You're forgetting that we've got these." I took out my badge. "All we have to do is ask."

We flashed our badges at the post office and

were taken to the supervisor, who was in the back of the building, in the vast mail-sorting area, overseeing the individual carriers as they gathered letters and parcels they had to deliver.

The supervisor's name was Kathy Lopez. She was a heavy woman with an almost military bearing who wore her uniform with obvious pride.

I tried to channel Mariska Hargitay's tough, world-weary attitude on *Law & Order.*

"I'm Natalie Teeger and this is Adrian Monk. We're with the Summit Police Department."

She nodded and put her hands on her hips. "Zip 07901."

"That's right," I said, though I had no clue if it was or not. "We've got some questions we'd like to ask Irwin Deeb. What zip code can we find him in?"

"In 96761," she said. "Or maybe 89109."

"Maui or Las Vegas," Monk said.

Lopez looked at him with admiration. "You're good. Have you worked in the postal service?"

"No, I'm just a literate citizen, of which there appear to be few."

"Amen, brother."

"What makes you think Deeb is in Hawaii or Nevada?" I asked.

276

"He's always talked about going to those places and he's got a whole bunch of vacation days saved up. Two weeks ago he took them. He won't be back for another week."

"We think that he never left San Francisco," I said, "and that he's actually been squatting in empty homes on his route."

"That's seriously creepy. Why would Irwin do that?"

"It's complicated," I said.

"Is he a sexual deviant?"

"I don't think so," I said. "Why do you ask that?"

"Because squatting in people's empty houses sounds like a sexually deviant thing to do. Does he do strange things with their underwear?"

"Underwear is not part of this investigation," I said.

"Thank God," Monk said.

"You might want to make it part of it."

"We'll take that under advisement," I said. "Can you give us a list of current vacation mail holds filed by residents on his route?"

"Sure," she said. "What about their shoes? Does he do strange things with them?"

The first two homes we visited were empty and showed no signs of break-ins. However, the third house had been broken into and trashed inside. We were careful not to touch anything and I was relieved not to find any bodies. The next house appeared empty and secure. But there were fresh footprints in the mud under the windows, as if someone else had been scoping out the house recently.

Not everything about Monk's solution to the mystery was adding up for me, so I mentioned my concerns to him on our way to the fourth house on our list.

"A few things about this whole case just don't make sense to me. I'm not close with my mailman, but I have known him casually for years. I suppose Irwin could have gone to Salvatore Lucarelli with a plan for stealing the marked money, or vice versa, but I just can't picture him killing Jeroen Berge with a karate kick to the face."

"I'm not saying that he did," Monk said, plucking more dog hair from my clothes.

I swatted his hand away. "Would you please stop picking at me with those tweezers?"

"I'm sure that he's probably not in this alone," Monk said, ignoring my request. I was driving, so I was at a disadvantage for fending him off. "He could be working with Lucarelli, or with a crooked FBI agent, or with them both. All I know is that he's been staying in empty homes."

"That's the other thing. Why is he doing that? I mean, wouldn't it have made more sense, and drawn less attention to himself, if he'd just gone along with his everyday life?"

"Maybe he is. Maybe he's been occupying empty houses for years. We won't know until we find him."

If that was true, then Kathy Lopez was right and Irwin was one seriously creepy guy.

But did that also make him a killer?

The fourth house was at the end of a cul-de-sac on a steep hill that overlooked my street. It was basically a bungalow, hardly a thousand square feet, with shingled siding and lots of overgrown juniper hedges — tangled with spiderwebs — close to the walls. A cracked concrete driveway led to a tiny ramshackle detached garage in the backyard.

We stepped up to the front door. Monk crouched down and studied the doorknob.

"The lock has been picked," Monk said. "Just like yours. Look at the lateral scratches."

"I'll take your word for it. I'm going around back. After a minute or two, knock on the door and announce that we're here."

I ran in a low crouch, below the line of the windows, along the driveway.

If we'd been full-fledged cops, with guns to go along with our badges, I would have drawn my weapon. So when I spotted a rusty shovel leaning against the garage, I grabbed it to use just in case Irwin was hanging out with the martial artist who kicked Jeroen Berge into the afterlife.

I crouched beside a juniper bush and waited. A few moments later I heard Monk knock on the door.

"This is the police. Irwin Deeb, if you are in there, please come out with your hands up."

I heard something squeak inside the house. It sounded to me like mattress or couch cushion springs being relieved of weight. Then I heard scrambling footsteps.

Staying low, below the top of the juniper hedge, I followed the sounds to a window, which I heard being jimmied up.

I stood up to see Irwin Deeb in his blue mailman's uniform, his mailbag slung over his shoulder, trying to squirm out the window. It was a tight squeeze because this postman was built more like Kevin James than Kevin Costner.

Irwin landed on the junipers, sinking deep into the prickly branches before extricating himself, only to find me standing there, shaking my head.

"Hello, Irwin," I said.

Needless to say, he was startled. But to my surprise, I detected something else.

Relief.

"Ms. Teeger! What are you doing here?"

"You first," I said, setting the shovel aside. I didn't think he'd be slaying me with a karate kick.

Irwin stood up, brushed himself off, and straightened his uniform with a couple of tugs.

"I'm house-sitting for my good friend Ted Bowers."

"Like you were for me?"

He blushed, his round cheeks turning bright red. By now, Monk was coming up behind me, carefully avoiding the cracks in the sidewalk.

Irwin looked past me at Monk. "You aren't the police. I know you. You're Adrian Monk, Ms. Teeger's boss. What's going on here?"

I flashed my badge, mostly because I loved doing it whenever I could. "Actually, Irwin, we are police officers, back in Summit, New Jersey, and I didn't appreciate coming home to a dead body in my bathtub and thousands of dollars in stolen money under my bed.

And I'm sure Jeroen Berge didn't appreciate getting killed."

"What?" Irwin said, taking a step back. "Mr. Berge is dead? Oh my God, not him, too."

"Is that your way of saying you didn't kill him?"

"I didn't kill Mr. Berge. He was a great guy. I used to read his *Playboy*s all the time."

"So you really are a sexual deviant," Monk said.

"I used to read his *Architectural Digest*s, too. Free access to all kinds of magazines is one of the perks of my job. Shoot me for trying to intellectually enrich myself."

"I don't care about the magazines you read," I said. "What I want to know is who killed Jeroen Berge."

"Obviously, they did," Irwin said. "I thought you were them coming after me. That's why I was escaping out the window."

"Who are they?" Monk asked.

"I have no idea," Irwin said. "All I know is that they want me dead."

CHAPTER TWENTY-THREE: MR. MONK GOES POSTAL

"Gee, do you think it might have something to do with the five hundred thousand dollars in marked money that you stole from the FBI evidence room?" I asked.

"Is that where it came from?" Irwin said. "Oh my God, this is even worse than I thought."

Monk tipped his head and regarded Irwin at an angle. "You didn't steal the money."

"Of course not," Irwin said. "I'm not a thief."

"Then where did you get it?"

"I was delivering a Priority Mail package to one of those mailbox outfits when I tripped and dropped it. The box split open on the curb and when I bent down to pick it up, I saw that it was stuffed with cash, enough to give me the chance to live the life I always dreamed of. I saw it as divine providence."

"Who was the box addressed to?" Monk asked.

"John Smith," Irwin said. "I didn't have to be a detective to figure out the money was probably stolen. I figured it would serve the guy right if somebody stole the money from him. It's almost poetic justice."

"First it was divine providence and now poetic justice," I said. "You're just full of rationalizations for what you did."

"Okay, it was like winning the lottery. Can you blame me for seeing it as an opportunity? I'm a dedicated public servant who has never gotten a fair deal once in his life," Irwin said. "Not even now."

"I still don't understand what you were doing in my house," I said.

"I went to work the next day, like I hadn't found half a million dollars in cash, but when I came home that night, I saw someone ransacking my house. I knew that John Smith had found me and that I had to disappear fast."

"So you got the list of vacation mail holds along your route and hid out in the empty houses," Monk said. "That was very clever."

"Why didn't you just hop a plane to South America?" I asked.

"I don't speak Spanish, for one thing, and hot climates make me break out in hives."

"Okay," I said, restraining the urge to strangle him. "Why didn't you take a plane to Europe, or a bus to Canada, or just get in your car and drive?"

"Because that's exactly what they would expect me to do and they'd take appropriate measures. I was afraid they'd be watching the airports and bus stations, rental car agencies and borders. I figured do the opposite of what they would expect, and that way I'd improve my chances of not getting caught. So I decided to lay low somewhere they would never think to look for me. The last thing they would expect is for me to hide in plain sight, so to speak."

"How did you pick the locks on the houses?" Monk asked.

"I have a locksmith on my route and he subscribes to *National Locksmith, Locksmith Ledger,* and all the best magazines in the field," Irwin said. "I've never missed an issue."

"If you were so afraid of getting caught," I said, "why did you go to the Belmont bar?"

"I didn't think I'd be in any danger. I mean, who'd ever think to look for me there? I wanted to live large, drink expensive wine, and hang out with beautiful women, not sit in your house eating Cheetos."

"You ate my Cheetos?"

"I wasn't in the bar thirty seconds before the most beautiful woman in the place came over to me. One thing led to another, which almost never happens without some begging, and we went back to your place. It was the most glorious, exciting, and wildly erotic night of my life. But I underestimated them."

"What do you mean?" Monk asked.

"In the morning, I told Michelle how beautiful and special she was, and that if she'd let me, I'd treat her like a princess for the rest of her life, starting with a gourmet homemade breakfast. But you didn't have anything edible in your house."

"You didn't mind my Cheetos."

"She deserved better than that. So I told her to stay in bed while I went to the store. When I got back, I found her in the bathtub, murdered by John Smith. I was heartbroken, but I did the only thing I could do. I grabbed my money from under the bed and I ran." He looked down at his feet, ashamed. "It's my fault that she's dead."

"She wasn't murdered," Monk said. "She killed herself."

"I don't believe it. Why would she do that?" Irwin said. "She had everything to live for. She had me."

"We know that Michelle was deeply de-

286

pressed, that she hated her life," I said. "We'll never know exactly what was going through her mind that morning, but I think when she saw how sweet you were, and how wonderfully you were treating her, it made her feel terrible about herself. She couldn't live with the person she had become, which was nothing at all like the idealized woman you saw. So while you were out, she killed herself."

"I didn't idealize anything," Irwin said. "She was an angel."

"Michelle was a con artist," Monk said. "She picked up men for illicit sexual encounters, drugged their alcoholic beverages, and ran off with their money."

"She didn't drug me," he said.

"Michelle had five thousand dollars of your stolen money in her purse," I said. "So, at some point she was planning on robbing you, but something changed her mind."

"Self-loathing," Monk said.

"But I thought she was wonderful," Irwin said. "I told her so."

"I guess that wasn't enough," I said.

"So no one is after me?"

"Oh, they're after you, all right," I said. "The irony is that by killing herself, Michelle probably saved your life. It made you run before the bad guy was on your trail.

287

But he definitely is now. Jeroen Berge walked in on him."

"So she was an angel after all," Irwin said.

"I suppose she was," I said.

Monk believed that whoever stole the marked money was chasing the same trail that we were, only we lucked onto Irwin before the killer did.

I supposed the smart thing to do would have been to take Irwin straight to police headquarters, but we were still no closer to figuring out who the murderer was than we were before, though Monk had a theory behind the crime, which he explained as the three of us drove out to Tewksbury to find Yuki.

"Security going in and out of the Federal Building is tight, for employees and visitors," Monk said. "Nobody could walk out of there with five hundred thousand dollars in cash, and taking it out bit by bit over time would have been too risky. So they mailed it out."

"It's brilliant and gets bonus points for being simple," I said. "But that narrows down the suspects to any agent in the building with access to the evidence room."

Monk turned around and looked at Irwin. "We've only recovered ten thousand dollars.

What did you do with the rest of it?"

"I've got twenty thousand in my mailbag," Irwin said. "The rest is in the safest place on earth."

"Under a mattress?" I said.

"The United States Post Office," he said. "I filed a vacation hold before I left and mailed the money to myself. It's on a shelf where no one but me can get it without a search warrant."

We probably should have made a U-turn right then, gone back to the police station, and told the captain what we knew. Or, better yet, we should have called the FBI and let them know that we'd recovered their money.

It would have cleared my name and Monk's, but Irwin Deeb would likely face jail time and I wasn't so sure that was fair. And, to be honest, from an egotistical viewpoint, it wasn't enough for me that we recovered the money. I wanted to nail the bad guy, too.

So I kept driving to Tewksbury with no idea at all about what we were going to do with Irwin or how we'd flush out the killer.

But at least we'd be able to reunite Ambrose and Yuki and I took some satisfaction in that.

We didn't know who the guys were who

tried to grab Yuki, or what they wanted, but we knew she was hiding and we didn't want to spook her. And, on the off chance that the grocery store was still being watched, we parked on the other side of the storage facility, which was on the next block, and then we walked to the front gate.

There was no resident manager. The gate opened and closed using a key-card system and the fence was topped with razor wire, which had somehow snagged a few scraps of plastic wrap.

The three of us stood staring at the key-card unit as if our gazes alone would be enough to make it open.

"How are we going to get inside?" Monk asked.

"I could climb the fence, but that razor wire is a problem," I said.

"We could go to a hardware store, buy a tarp, and throw it over the wire to protect you from getting cut," Monk said.

"But we're out in the open here," I said. "Someone could see us and call the police."

"We are the police," Monk said.

"I don't think that's going to give us a free pass on breaking and entering."

"Technically, we aren't breaking or entering."

"Okay, criminal trespassing," I said.

Suddenly the gate hummed and slid open. Monk and I turned to see Irwin leaning against the key-card reader and smiling with pride. While Monk and I were arguing, Irwin had somehow managed to finesse the reader.

"How did you do that?" I asked.

"Same way I learned to pick locks," he said. "Being a mailman is a great way to educate yourself on a broad range of topics."

"Especially if you want to be a criminal," I said as I walked past him into the storage lot.

"I've also learned to crochet," Irwin said as he and Monk followed after me.

The three of us snaked our way around the boats, cars, horse trailers, Jet Skis, campers, and other large vehicles to Ambrose's motor home. The shades were closed on all of the windows and a curtain was drawn in front of the windshield.

I went up to the door and knocked, careful not to raise my voice too loud. "Yuki, it's Natalie Teeger and Adrian Monk. We're here to help you."

There was no sound from inside the trailer, no indication at all that it was occupied.

After a minute or two, Monk moved past

me and knocked again.

"This is Adrian Monk, Ambrose Monk's brother. I just want to state now, for the record, that I don't approve of your relationship with him. But he asked us to find you and we have. We know your real name is Erika Ito and that you have been hiding in this motor home since you were assaulted in the parking lot across the street. However, if you don't open this door promptly, we will call the police and report that my brother's motor home has been burglarized. Since you are a convicted felon, this offense could send you straight back to the big house, where you undoubtedly belong."

The door opened a crack. All I saw was darkness. I stepped up and pushed the door a bit more, sunshine spilling into the interior of the motor home to reveal Yuki in a shaft of light, crouched low by the driver's seat and aiming a .357 Magnum at us.

CHAPTER TWENTY-FOUR:
MR. MONK GOES BANANAS

I'd seen the gun before. It had belonged to Dub Clemens, the journalist that Yuki was working for when we met her on the road. And Monk had actually fired the gun to save his brother's life. But my familiarity with the weapon didn't make it any less unsettling to have it pointed at me.

"You can put the gun down," I said. "You're among friends."

She gestured with the gun to Irwin. "Who is he?"

"My mailman."

"We prefer the term *letter carrier*," Irwin said.

"Why did you bring him?" she asked.

"It's complicated," I replied. "The longer we stand here, the more likely we are to draw attention, and I think that's the last thing you want."

She stood up, but kept her gun trained on the open door. "Okay, you can come in, but do not open the door all the way, and lock it behind you once you are inside."

We slipped in one by one and she kept the gun aimed at the door in case some unseen assailant used the opportunity to dash in and kill her. I closed the door and locked it.

"Don't turn on the lights or open the blinds," Yuki said, putting her gun down on the dining table and taking a seat. The only light in the RV seeped in from around the edges of the blinds and the drapes across the windshield. But even in the semidarkness, I could see that she was exhausted. "How did you find me?"

I explained it all, then tried to reassure her. "I don't think you have to worry about anyone else finding you the same way we did. Nobody but Mr. Monk would ever notice the blinds."

"I hope you're right," she said.

Irwin and I sat down across the table from Yuki, and Monk stood, his arms crossed, striking a very judgmental posture.

"Who were those men who attacked you and what do they want?" he asked.

"They want the money I took from them and then they want me dead."

"Me, too! I've got exactly the same problem," Irwin said. "We've just met and we already have so much in common. Do you like to crochet?"

Yuki looked at me. "Who *is* this guy?"

"Irwin Deeb," I said, and then I told her my story of woe and stolen cash. When I was done, she just shook her head.

"Aren't we a lovely bunch," she said.

"But only one of us is a convicted felon," Monk said.

"Not true," I said.

"And a killer," he said.

"Again, not true," I said.

"You're reformed," Monk said.

"Maybe she is, too," I said and turned to her. "All we know is that you embezzled a million dollars from Juanita Banana Company."

"And killed someone," Monk quickly added, just in case I'd forgotten.

I gave Monk a sharp look, which I am not sure he could see in the dim light, and then turned back to Yuki. "Could you fill in the blanks for us?"

Yuki sighed. "I was an idealistic computer hacker living in St. Louis. I thought I could change the world with a few keystrokes. Juanita Banana paid the Marxist death squads in Urabá, Colombia, over a million dollars in protection money. It didn't matter to Juanita that the guerrillas were using that money to kill thousands of civilians,

295

crush labor unions, and drive peasants off of their land. All that mattered to them was keeping their business running smoothly. So I hacked into Juanita's payroll system and stole a million dollars, which I dispersed to dozens of human rights organizations to even the score."

"So Juanita alerted law enforcement and you became a fugitive from justice," Monk said.

Yuki laughed. "Juanita didn't call the police or the FBI, because that would have generated unwanted publicity and scrutiny. They called their own death squad, Blackthorn Security, the same people the U.S. government hired to commit their 'extraordinary renditions,' which is a ridiculously docile term for outright illegal kidnappings committed on foreign soil. One of those lovable Blackthorn guys attacked me on the street as I was coming out of a coffeehouse. I fought back, he lost his footing on a piece of uneven sidewalk, and I pushed him in front of a bus."

"This is why I keep saying that cracked sidewalks are a hazard," Monk said.

"Really?" I said. "Because you might trip while attacking a woman and fall under a bus?"

"If that sidewalk had been properly maintained, that man wouldn't be dead," Monk said.

"But I would be," Yuki said.

"You're missing my point," Monk said.

"You could learn a few things from Ambrose about empathy," Yuki said.

"He could learn a few things from me about not fornicating with tattooed, killer biker chicks."

Irwin looked at her. "Does this mean you've got a boyfriend?"

"Yes," she said.

"But we've got this amazing connection," he said.

"So what did you do after the guy was hit by the bus?" I asked her, eager to keep the conversation on track.

"I stuck around and waited for the police."

"You did?" Monk said.

"Of course I did," she said. "What kind of person do you think I am?"

"A tattooed, killer biker chick," Monk said.

"I wasn't any of those things at the time. I was an A student studying computer science at community college, I didn't have a single tattoo, and I drove a Ford Escort. I was an upstanding citizen who'd fought off an attacker. Naturally, I stayed because if I'd bolted, that would have been irresponsible and made an act of self-defense into a crime."

"It was," Monk said.

"The hacking was, technically speaking, but what happened to that Blackthorn agent was an accident. He brought it on himself. I figured, wrongly as it turned out, that no jury would ever convict me for that," she said. "Besides, I thought the police were the only ones who could protect me from Juanita Banana and Blackthorn."

"This is such a cool story," Irwin said. "It's *The Girl with the Dragon Tattoo,* except with bananas instead of Nazis."

"Didn't Juanita's actions in Colombia come out in the trial?" I asked. "It might have justified your actions."

She shook her head. "The judge ruled that bringing that issue into trial was prejudicial or irrelevant or some other crap and my public defender was too inexperienced to do anything about it. I was convicted of embezzlement and involuntary manslaughter and sent to prison. Juanita didn't even get a slap on the wrist."

"But they didn't get their money back," I said.

"That's because I refused to tell them where I'd sent it and I'd wiped all of my electronic footprints," she said. "But they were convinced I had it stashed somewhere. I knew they'd be waiting for me when I got out. So I looked at prison as another college and took unofficial courses in self-defense and falling off the grid."

Yuki went on to say that she changed her name and her appearance when she got out of prison and went to ground, emerging only to take a job working as journalist Dub Clemens' assistant. Clemens was dying of lung cancer and crisscrossing the country in an RV, chasing a story on an elusive serial killer.

The job offered her the perfect way to stay out of sight and off the grid, traveling the back roads of America completely unnoticed.

As far as Juanita Banana was concerned, she'd disappeared from the face of the earth.

"But then I met Ambrose, moved in with him as his assistant, and got sloppy. I forgot I was a hunted woman and how resourceful Blackthorn is," she said. "The other day, they found me and attempted an 'extraordinary rendition,' but I guess they didn't do enough research on me. They didn't know that I got a prison black belt."

She smiled with pride. Wiping the parking lot with the Blackthorn ops was apparently a pleasant memory.

"What are you still doing here?" Monk asked. "Why haven't you run?"

"Because I love your brother, you idiot," Yuki said.

"It's probably a good idea to have someone on tap as a backup in case it doesn't work out," Irwin said. "Someone who really understands what you are going through right now."

"And that would be you," Yuki said.

"I know what you're feeling," Irwin said. "I share your isolation, your fear, your pain under the yoke of injustice. Great relationships have been built on far less."

"The yoke of injustice?" I said.

"You'd have to be in our shoes to understand," Irwin said, reaching out to touch Yuki.

"If your hand touches me, I will break it," she said.

He withdrew it. "You can see how emotionally scarred she is already."

Monk groaned. "If you really cared about Ambrose, you'd go and take the danger that follows you as far away from him as you can get."

"I would, but it's not that simple," she said. "I know that they are watching him and I'm afraid of what they might do to him if they get frustrated about not being able to find me. They might think that hurting him will bring me back."

And they'd be right, because even the thought that they might harm him was keeping her close by. Maybe they knew that might happen, too. "How do you know they are watching him?"

"Twenty-twenty hindsight and a quick recon under cover of darkness," she said. "A new family moved in across the street a week or so ago. And ever since, there have been a lot of cable, telephone, and electrical service trucks in the neighborhood. Obviously, it was Blackthorn setting up shop for round-the-clock surveillance."

"Or you have a vivid imagination," Monk said.

"I didn't imagine getting grabbed at the grocery store," Yuki said. "How do you think they knew I'd be there with enough notice to get there ahead of me?"

I'd had the same question when I watched the surveillance video. Now she'd answered it.

"So what's the plan?" Irwin asked. "We all hide out here until my bad guys and her bad guys give up and go away?"

That was my initial plan, but it didn't seem like a great long-term strategy.

"Because if it is," Irwin continued, "I'm

game. I can teach Yuki to crochet."

"I would rather give myself up to Blackthorn and let them torture me to death," Yuki said.

I thought about the similarities of their plight and then, out of nowhere, a plan came to me almost fully formed. It was risky, and there were a thousand ways it could go wrong, but there was one aspect to it that was too appealing to ignore, so I led with that.

"My plan is to kill two birds with one stone," I said.

"That's a terrible plan," Monk said.

"You haven't even heard it yet," I said.

"It would be much better to kill two birds with two stones," Monk said.

"I think you're missing the point of the analogy," Irwin said. "Killing two birds with one stone refers to accomplishing multiple goals with one action."

"You could kill four birds with two stones," Monk said. "That would be a good plan."

"Forget about the birds," I said. "I am sorry I even mentioned birds. For this plan to work, we're going to need to borrow a mail delivery truck. Can you get us one, Irwin?"

"No problem," Irwin said. "I have many

brothers in the international fraternity of letter carriers."

"Great, now all we need is a script, clockwork timing, this gun, and a lot of luck."

"And two stones," Monk said. "Or four."

"Forget the stones. There are no stones involved." I shifted my gaze between Yuki and Irwin. "If this works, neither one of you will have to be on the run any longer. But I won't lie to you — this plan will put you both in serious danger."

"I'm tired of hiding," Irwin said.

"Me, too," Yuki said.

"We're in this together," Irwin said. "To the bitter end."

"Yours is going to come immediately if you don't stop hitting on me," she said to him, then looked back at me. "Tell me what you've got in mind."

CHAPTER TWENTY-FIVE:
MR. MONK AND THE PLAN

It had been only a day or so since Ambrose asked us to look for Yuki, but he told me later that it felt to him like it had been weeks. He paced around the house and kept peeking out the windows, hoping to see Yuki returning. But all he saw was the cable installers and phone repair trucks coming and going across the street.

The way he explained it to me, he'd always felt safe, warm, and comfortable in his home, but ever since Yuki left, he felt trapped. Before she came into his life, there really wasn't anything outside his door that he wanted.

Out there were chaos, uncertainty, feces, crowds, unpredictability, wild animals, uncertain borders, billions of insects, automobile traffic, germs, birds — all of which added up to inconceivable dangers and constant risk across an incalculable vastness topped by an endless sky.

It was a space he couldn't wrap his mind around. Just thinking about it made him break out in a sweat.

His house was the opposite of all that.

The walls and the roof created defined boundaries, safety, calm, certainty, isolation, normalcy, and predictability. He had almost total control over his environment. He could visualize it, know it, and master it.

But now she was out there somewhere and he was inside and that was unbearable.

Even if he could go outside, he wouldn't know where to look for her, and that was if he could somehow shut out all the distractions, all the chaos, all the unknowns.

And the whole time he was out there, he'd be afraid that while he was gone, she'd come back and leave again because he wasn't there like he was supposed to be.

It reminded him of how he'd felt those first few years, even that first long decade, after his father went out for Chinese food and didn't come back. Ambrose's biggest fear was that whatever he'd done that drove his father away had now scared Yuki off, too.

It took thirty years for his dad to finally come back. He prayed that she would return to him sooner than that.

Ambrose tried to distract himself from his

fears and worries by working on his latest assignment — writing an owner's manual for an electronic rice cooker that was so advanced it also connected to the home wireless network and could be programmed from afar with a smartphone application.

But his muse had abandoned him when Yuki left. His writing was flat, sterile, passionless. He couldn't seem to find his voice, or to capture the character of the rice cooker and, with it, the life-changing potential that it offered to the consumer.

It suddenly struck him that his life without Yuki was like trying to cook rice without water: dry and unfulfilled.

No wonder he couldn't write the manual.

There was a knock at the door. It was a sound that always made him nervous, since it meant he had to breach the security of his home to let someone, or something, from out there gain access to him and his safe little world.

But it could be Yuki.

Then again, she wouldn't knock — she would just come in.

So who was it?

Ambrose crept up and peered through the peephole. He saw a cherubic mailman and a U.S. Postal Service truck parked at the curb. This was Irwin Deeb, but Ambrose didn't know him, of course, at the time.

The mailman held a Priority Mail flat-rate envelope, which made Ambrose happy.

Ambrose liked Priority Mail flat-rate envelopes because he didn't have to calculate postage no matter what he put in them. He also liked having them around. There was something remarkable and comforting about an item that managed to stay the same even as it changed. So he kept a minimum of one hundred Priority Mail flat-rate envelopes in a drawer of his desk at all times just because it made him feel good.

He opened the door. "Yes?"

"Are you Ambrose Monk?" Irwin asked.

"You must be new. Who else would be here?"

"I have a package for you," the mailman said and handed it to him.

"How come it wasn't delivered with my regular mail?"

"It came in after your postal carrier left," the mailman said. "Have a good day."

The mailman turned and hurried back to his truck. That's when Ambrose noticed the Priority Mail envelope was just like all the others in his drawer — missing stamps and a postmark.

That made no sense at all.

Why was the mailman delivering a Priority Mail envelope that hadn't been posted?

Ambrose was about to call out to the mail-man when he noticed something else.

The address was in Yuki's handwriting.

When he looked up again, the mail truck was already driving way.

Stunned, Ambrose closed the door, locked it and bolted it, then took the envelope to the dining room, placed it on the table, and sat down in front of it.

This was all very odd.

He pulled open the tab and removed four crisp sheets of paper, all written in Yuki's handwriting.

One appeared to be a letter and the other three looked like pages from a handwritten screenplay.

He read the letter:

Ambrose,

Do not read this letter out loud. Your house is under visual and audio surveillance by very bad people from my past who tried to abduct me at the grocery store. They are in the house and service vehicles across the street.

Do not spy on them, but do keep compulsively looking out the window for me. You have to act as if nothing has changed.

I am safe. Adrian and Natalie are with

me and we have a plan that we hope will make everything right so that I can come home again.

I am going to call you in one hour. I have enclosed a script for our phone conversation. It is very important that you follow the script word for word, since they will be listening.

Please know that I love you, that I am nearby, and that I will never leave you.

Love,
Yuki

Ambrose read the letter twice and when he was done, he realized that he was crying tears of joy.

Yuki called Ambrose precisely one hour later from my car where we were parked on Golden Gate Avenue, just east of Hyde in San Francisco. She used a throwaway cell phone that we bought at a convenience store and we put the conversation on speaker so we could all hear it.

This is the script that they performed, and quite dramatically, too:

Ambrose: Greetings, you've reached the home of Ambrose Monk. Ambrose Monk speaking.

Yuki: It's me.

Ambrose: Where are you? What happened?

Yuki: My past caught up with me. A long time ago I stole a lot of money from some very bad people and stashed it away. They want it back.

Ambrose: So give it to them.

Yuki: I can't. It's gone beyond that now. They also want me dead. I'm calling to say good-bye.

Ambrose: Please don't go. We can figure this out.

Yuki: I already have. I'm going to use the money to start a new life in another country, long enough to get plastic surgery and create a bulletproof identity. When I'm done, nobody will know that I was ever Japanese.

Ambrose: They'll catch you if you try to go back to St. Louis for the money.

Yuki: I don't have to, it's right here in San Francisco. The money was in a box I stowed with friends. They had no idea what was inside. A few weeks ago, I had them send it to me at a post office in the city. I told them I was a student now at Hastings.

Ambrose: What if whoever is chasing you knows about the package?

Yuki: I am sending a stranger in to get it for me, then meeting him in the alley in back.

Ambrose: It sounds dangerous. I don't like it.

Yuki: I don't, either. But I promise this isn't the end. It's a beginning.

Ambrose: It feels like the end to me.

Yuki: Someday a woman you don't recognize is going to come up to you, give you a kiss, and whisper that she loves you. That woman will be me.

Yuki hangs up.

It was a powerful scene, and all of us but Monk had tears in our eyes when it was over. Irwin actually applauded.

The emotion Yuki and Ambrose brought to the scene was palpable, probably because the words and the sentiments behind them weren't too far away from what both of them were actually feeling.

And I am not just saying that because I wrote the little play, with input from Yuki and Monk, of course.

The post office where Irwin got his mail was on Golden Gate Avenue and Hyde, across from the University of California's Hastings College of Law.

We figured it would be too on-the-nose to

mention the street that the post office was on in the conversation, so we dropped in a mention of Hastings instead for Blackthorn to work with.

I wanted to invest Blackthorn in the story. I was hoping that if they had to deduce where the post office was, they'd be so busy flattering themselves for their cleverness that they wouldn't stop to think that maybe they were being manipulated. I also hoped they would be able to triangulate where the cell phone call originated, which would help them pinpoint the post office, which was right across the street from where we were parked.

Monk's contributions included writing Ambrose's greeting and constantly checking the word count. He was pleased because the final draft of the script was 290 words, 1,182 characters, and 1,460 characters if we included the spaces between words, all even numbers, a balance we achieved thanks to some judicious trimming.

"I think you have a future as a writer," Monk said.

"What would I write about?" I said. "My life isn't that interesting."

"Mine is," Monk said.

It was something to think about.

The post office was a one-story, virtually

windowless concrete block on the northeast corner of Golden Gate Avenue and Hyde Street that looked like a remodeled mausoleum which, architecturally speaking, made it fit in perfectly with the Hastings College of Law monoliths that were on two of the opposite corners.

Golden Gate Avenue was a one-way street with the traffic heading eastbound. Hyde was a one-way street with southbound traffic. We were parked facing the intersection and directly across the street from the mouth of the alley behind the post office.

The alley didn't cut clear across the block to Turk Street to the north. Instead, it formed an L, opening on Larkin to the west instead, which meant that Monk and I couldn't see what was going on at the other end of the alley. But I suspected a black panel van would soon be parking on the Larkin side and another would soon be showing up near us.

Irwin had changed into street clothes, sunglasses, and a baseball cap that I'd picked up for him on the cheap at the same Marshalls I went to the other day. Now that he was out of his uniform, I didn't think anybody would recognize him as the mailman who went to Ambrose's door.

Immediately after the call, Irwin and Yuki

got out of the car and walked over to the Allstars Donuts and Burgers, on the north-east corner of Golden Gate and Hyde, to have a cup of coffee and give all the players in the game time to get into position.

Sure enough, a few minutes later a black panel van with tinted windows parked in a red zone just a few yards behind us.

I took out my cell phone and made calls to Yuki and two other people, and then took out the gun and put it in my lap in case my timing was off and things went very wrong.

"Are you sure this is going to work?" Monk asked.

"Not at all," I said.

"So you're racked with anxiety, self-doubt, inadequacy, and facing the prospect of im-minent doom."

"That about sums it up."

"Now you know how I've felt every day since I was born," Monk said. "Actually, since shortly before my birth. I dreaded the birth canal."

"How can you possibly know that?"

"Because I've been suffering from PTSD ever since."

That's when Irwin Deeb emerged from the restaurant. We watched him in silence as he crossed the street and entered the post office to claim his vacation hold mail.

I took a deep breath.

The game was about to begin. I just prayed it wouldn't end with anybody getting killed.

Chapter Twenty-Six:
Mr. Monk and the Sting

It was a tense and seemingly endless few minutes as Irwin waited in line inside the post office and the Blackthorn operatives, in the van behind us, waited for Yuki to appear and go into the alley.

I was certain that they had spotted her in the restaurant by now, especially since she was sitting at a window booth so that she'd be seen, but they were holding off on making a move because they wanted to catch her with the money in hand.

And we wanted that, too.

So we were all showing commendable restraint.

Irwin emerged from the side entrance of the post office holding a large brown cardboard box sealed with an overabundance of packing tape. He obviously didn't want to take any chances that this box of money would split open the way the other one had.

"Here we go," I said, taking out my badge

and putting it on a lanyard around my neck.

Monk wouldn't wear his badge on a lanyard since there was no way to keep it centered on his chest at all times.

Irwin stepped into the alley and waited. Yuki came out of the restaurant, crossed the street, and headed for the alley. I noted a man in a suit rounding the corner at Hyde and falling into step behind her. At the same time another man, wearing jogging shorts and supposedly listening to an iPod, came around the corner at Larkin and walked toward her.

They were boxing her in.

Yuki pretended not to notice, but I knew that she did.

I glanced in the rearview mirror and saw that the driver of the van was already turning his wheels toward the alley in preparation for the grab.

This was going to happen fast. I started the car, released the brake, and put the gear into drive.

Yuki stepped into the alley, traded some small talk with Irwin, then took the package from him. She started toward the sidewalk and the two men grabbed her, the guy in the suit jabbing her with a Taser.

Irwin bolted down the alley. He wasn't being a coward. He'd been specifically instructed not to attempt to rescue her. We wanted her captured.

But the Taser wasn't part of the plan.

The van shot across the street — nearly causing two collisions with oncoming vehicles — and blocked the entrance to the alley. I couldn't see what was happening, but I was certain that the two men heaved Yuki's limp body and the money inside the van and climbed aboard themselves, sliding the door shut behind them.

The abduction was over in less than thirty seconds.

I pulled out in front of the van, getting a head start on it as it sped off. Just before the intersection, I yanked the wheel hard to the left, fishtailing the car directly across the van's path, giving the driver no time to veer around me.

The van skidded to a stop, burning rubber and creating a screech that sounded like Godzilla's fingernails on an enormous chalkboard, raising goose bumps all over my body.

I swung my door open, stepped out in a firing stance, and aimed my gun at the driver.

"Police! Get out of the vehicle with your hands up!"

I guess I wasn't very convincing, because

the driver sneered at me, put the vehicle in reverse, and floored it.

The van's tires squealed against the asphalt as it backed up at high speed.

On a one-way street.

The cars behind the van swerved wildly to avoid collisions, sideswiping parked vehicles on both sides of the street.

It was ugly.

People on the sidewalks screamed, flattening themselves against the buildings and ducking into alcoves. It was a miracle that nobody got hurt.

Monk got out of the car and looked at me over the hood. "Was this part of the plan?"

"It's evolving," I said, my back to him, my eyes still on the van as it retreated toward Larkin. I could hear sirens approaching from somewhere.

Monk ran to the corner. If I'd been smart, I would have done the same and got off the street.

But I stood my ground in a firing stance. I was debating whether to shoot, and was an instant away from having to make a decision when two black-and-white police cars and Captain Stottlemeyer's Crown Vic raced across Larkin.

The cop cars came to a screeching stop in the intersection, creating a barrier behind the van, which skidded to a jarring halt just shy of rear-ending them.

Captain Stottlemeyer had been my first call after the one to Yuki. But my timing had been off. It took the police longer to show up than I'd anticipated.

But it had all worked out. The van was now trapped between the cop cars behind it and us in front. It wasn't going anywhere, Yuki was safe, and the money had been recovered.

The plan had worked.

More or less.

As for the second Blackthorn vehicle, the one I assumed had blocked the other end of the alley on Larkin, it was probably long gone, the operatives rushing back to Tewksbury to evacuate the house they were occupying before the authorities arrived.

It didn't matter. It was all over now.

I took a few steps toward the van to make my arrest, but then I saw its back wheels spin, kicking up smoke.

Oh hell.

The van roared toward me like a race car just leaving the starting line.

"Shoot!" Monk yelled from the sidewalk.

I thought about it as the van bore down on me. I wasn't the world's greatest shot, or even the world's 150,000th greatest shot, and Yuki was in that van.

Did I really want to take the chance that a stray bullet might find her?

I didn't.

So at the last second, I dove out of the way.

The actors on TV shows always make dives look so smooth and graceful. What they leave out is that when you are diving onto rough asphalt, and you aren't a professional stuntman who knows how to land and roll, and there's no pad to cushion your fall, it's a hard, painful, and bloody impact.

I am not a professional stuntman.

And I certainly didn't have a pad.

I hit the ground hard, lost my grip on my gun, and rolled up against a parked car just as the van T-boned my Buick and plowed it right through the window of Allstars Donuts and Burgers.

I never liked the Buick much, but I felt bad for the restaurant. Luckily, the few patrons in the place managed to scramble out of the way and were unharmed by the car that landed in their lunch.

That's when two black Suburbans skidded to a stop on either side of the van and half a dozen guys in blue Windbreakers with FBI written in big yellow letters on the back jumped out, guns drawn, led by Special

Agents Thorpe and Cardea.

Kidnapping is a federal offense, which was why my second call after the one to Yuki had been to the feds to report that their stolen money was on the move.

The feds also arrived later than I'd expected.

So much for my precision timing.

I made a vow to myself that the next time that I came up with a scheme to nail a team of crack private security agents for kidnapping, and clear me and Monk of a crime, and recover money stolen from an FBI evidence room, I would make my calls to law enforcement for backup a lot earlier.

I reached under the parked car for my gun and realized that my hands were scraped and bleeding. The knees of my jeans were torn, but that only made them look more stylish.

Monk and Irwin rushed over and helped me to my feet.

"You were incredible," Irwin said.

"That was one of the dumbest things you've ever done," Monk said. "But I'll have to check my list at home to find out where exactly this one ranks."

"You've kept a list?" I said.

"I keep a list of everything." Monk handed me a wipe. Stupidly, I used it on my hands.

322

It stung worse than scraping them did.

"We should go out for coffee sometime," Irwin said.

"Oh, come on, Irwin," I said, shaking my hands, hoping that would make the sting go away. "Do you really think that this is the best time to hit on me?"

"We've bonded in the heat of battle," he said.

I checked the intersection. The FBI agents had the van surrounded. Four Blackthorn guys came out with their hands on their heads and, wisely, so did Yuki.

More cop cars pulled up behind the FBI vehicles and officers ran into the restaurant to make sure nobody was hurt. Beyond them, I could see a paramedic unit, a fire truck, and an ambulance heading our way.

"Excuse me, gentlemen, I've still got a job to do." I held up my badge and headed into the intersection. "I'm Officer Natalie Teeger, Summit Police Department, and you're all under arrest for kidnapping, resisting arrest, assaulting a police officer, reckless driving, and general bad behavior." I looked over at Thorpe and gestured to Yuki. "She's the victim. You can let her go."

"Where's the money?" Thorpe asked.

"It's in the van," I said. "The brown box."

Cardea climbed into the van and tore

open the box, exposing the neatly wrapped stacks of cash.

"This is all a big misunderstanding," said the guy who'd Tasered Yuki. "We're security professionals, she's a thief, and that's stolen money that we've recovered."

"Yes, it is," I said. "From the FBI evidence room."

"What?" he said, stunned.

That's when Yuki, in one lightning move, reached under the man's jacket, grabbed his Taser, and zapped him with it, bringing him to his knees before Thorpe snatched the device from her.

"Stings, doesn't it?" she said and gave the Blackthorn guy a kick for good measure, then moved over to us.

Stottlemeyer and Devlin walked into the intersection. Devlin looked around at the destruction and nodded approvingly.

"I have to admit that I'm impressed, Teeger. This is the kind of crazy, jackass dangerous thing I might have done to make a major arrest."

"Thank you," I said.

"I wouldn't take that as a compliment," Monk said. "I'd look at it as a wake-up call."

"You might have brought us into this a little earlier," Stottlemeyer said to me.

I nodded. "At least ten minutes earlier."

"I was thinking before you made the decision to pull this crazy stunt in the first place," Stottlemeyer said.

Cardea brought a stack of the money over to Thorpe to examine. "It's definitely our cash."

Thorpe looked at it, then glared at me. "Are you going to tell us what the hell is going on here? When you called, you promised us our money and the man who had it, not a demolition derby."

"Special Agent Thorpe," I said, "meet U.S. Postal Carrier Irwin Deeb."

Irwin offered his hand. "Always a pleasure to meet another officer of the federal government."

Thorpe ignored the outstretched hand and looked at me. "What does he have to do with anything?"

"He recovered your money," Monk said.

"I don't understand," Thorpe said.

"Whoever stole it from the evidence room sent it to a mailbox service," Monk said. "Irwin happened to be the postal carrier delivering the box, which he accidentally dropped. The box broke open, he saw the cash, and he gave in to temptation."

"For which I am deeply sorry and ashamed," Irwin said.

"In return for his valor today," I said, "I'm

recommending that he get immunity from prosecution for whatever slight transgressions he might have committed along the way."

"You are?" Thorpe said with a derisive little snort. "How beneficent of you."

"What about his coconspirator, the one who stole the money from the evidence room?" Cardea said. "You think we should give him a free ride, too?"

"I had nothing to do with the theft," Irwin said.

"So you claim," Cardea said. "How do we know you aren't working for Salvatore Lucarelli?"

"Agent Cardea has a point, Natalie," Stottlemeyer said. "Does that immunity you're proposing extend to Jeroen Berge's murder as well?"

"Who is Jeroen Berge?" Thorpe asked, scratching his hand.

"It's going to take us some time to explain everything," Monk said. "And you're going to need a couple of hours to sort through all of this mess."

"Which she caused," Thorpe said, pointing a finger accusingly at me.

"She certainly did," Monk said. "I suggest that we all continue this conversation at the Federal Building when you're done here."

"Oh really?" Thorpe said. "And where the hell do you think you're going?"

The same question occurred to me, too.

"We're taking Yuki home," Monk said and looked at me. "Aren't we?"

"Yes, Mr. Monk, we are," I said, proud of him for putting his brother's interests, and his heart, before everything else. When it came down to it, Monk usually did the right thing. But then it occurred to me there was one big obstacle remaining. "As soon as we get a ride."

"You're not going anywhere," Thorpe said.

Stottlemeyer tossed a set of keys to me. "Use my car. Amy will go along with you and take Yuki's statement on the way. But the mailman stays with us."

"Thank you, Leland," I said.

"I'm not doing this for you," he said. "I'm doing it for Ambrose. I haven't decided yet whether to congratulate you or arrest you for what you did here."

Stottlemeyer turned his back on me and walked away, taking Irwin with him. Devlin gave me a smile.

"That's high praise in my book," she said.

Monk looked at me. "It's a bad book."

"I was on the force for years before my commanding officer told me that he couldn't decide whether to take my badge or give me commendation," she said. "As far as I'm concerned, you just became a real cop."

Oddly enough, I was flattered. I had no idea her approval meant anything to me. But it did.

"Give me the keys and I'll get the car," she said.

I gave them to her and she headed off.

Yuki came over to me, looked as if she was about to say something, and then just gave me a hug instead.

Monk frowned with disapproval.

"Juanita Banana and Blackthorn will go down in a big way for this," Yuki said. "I'll never have to worry about them again."

"That was the plan," I said. "Well, half of it anyway."

"I owe you one," she said, letting go of me.

"Make Ambrose happy," I said, "and we're even."

Monk shook his head.

"What?" I said. "Do you have a problem with that?"

"You shouldn't have let her hug you," Monk said.

"Why not?" Yuki said. "Is there a law against simple human contact?"

"Because now you're covered with dog

hair, too," he said, and plucked a hair off of her with his tweezers.

"Stop that," Yuki said, backing away.

"You'll thank me later," Monk said. He held the hair up in front of him, cocked his head, and studied it. The hair was white.

"What's wrong?" I asked.

But he didn't answer. He put the hair in a baggie, labeled it with a pen, and stuck it in his pocket. I was about to repeat the question, but that's when Devlin drove up in Stottlemeyer's car.

"You drive," Devlin said to me, getting out of the car and leaving the engine running. She pointed to Yuki. "You sit in the back with me and tell me all about what happened."

CHAPTER TWENTY-SEVEN:
MR. MONK AND
THE PERFECT MEAL

The ride into Marin County was long, since we got stuck in rush-hour traffic, but it gave Devlin all the time she needed to get Yuki's story.

I explained how we found Yuki and I gave Devlin the Web address so she could see the surveillance video of Blackthorn's first abduction attempt.

"Juanita Banana should have been satisfied when you were sent to prison," Devlin said. "Chasing you all these years, and the legal fees they are about to incur, are going to cost them a lot more than what you stole."

"They are a billion-dollar company with interests all over the world," Yuki said. "The cost means nothing to them. They wanted to send a message to anyone else who might dare to expose their greed and their avarice."

"They're sending one," I said. "But it's not the one they intended."

When I pulled up to the curb in front of Ambrose's house, I noticed there were no service vehicles around and the home across the street appeared to be empty. Blackthorn hadn't wasted any time closing down their operation and evacuating their team.

"This is where you grew up?" Devlin said, looking at the Monk family home.

"Yes, it is," Monk said. "Why do you sound so surprised?"

"It looks so normal," Devlin said.

"What were you expecting?" I asked.

"An institution," she said.

The front door of the house opened and I saw Ambrose framed in the doorway.

The four of us emerged from the car all at once and then something extraordinary happened. As soon as Ambrose spotted Yuki, he burst out of the house.

He leaped off the porch, ran down the front walk, and flew into her open arms, nearly tackling her.

They embraced for a long moment, Ambrose holding her tight, as if she were a life preserver and he might drown if he let go.

I glanced at Monk, and saw him staring at his brother in disbelief, his head cocked at an angle.

Ambrose kissed Yuki all over her face, making her giggle like a child. Then he took a step back, his hands still clutching her shoulders, and looked at her.

"You're so beautiful," he said. "And you're back."

"You came outside," she said, tears streaming down her cheeks.

"I want to be wherever you are, though I'd prefer if that was indoors," he said. "Did you mean what you wrote in your letter?"

"What part?"

"The part where you said that you'd never leave me?"

"Of course I did," she said.

Ambrose let go of her, took a deep breath, and dropped to one knee. "Then I would deeply appreciate it if you would consider the remote possibility of maybe marrying me at some point in the future, if you have no other options."

He reached into the pocket of his cardigan sweater and held out a blue plastic ring with a brown treasure chest on it as the setting. She took the ring and got down on her knees in front of him.

I felt like we should go, that we were intruding on their moment, but I couldn't move. Monk was as transfixed as I was. Devlin was watching the whole scene with an expression of bewilderment.

Yuki looked at the ring. "What is this?"

332

"A Cap'n Crunch ring," he said. "I've been saving it for you since 1965. The lid opens."

"It's wonderful," she said and slipped it on her finger.

"So will you think about my proposal?"

She shook her head. "No, Ambrose, I won't."

He nodded and started to get up. "It's okay, I understand. No offense taken."

Yuki grabbed his arm. "I don't need to think about it. The answer is yes."

He looked down at her in shock. "Would you mind repeating that, just for the record?"

She stood up, put her arms around him, and laid her head against his chest.

"Yes, I will marry you, Ambrose Monk. Now. Tomorrow. A year from now. Whenever and wherever you want. I am yours."

Ambrose smiled and now he looked at Monk. "Did you hear that, Adrian? She said yes. You're my witness."

For a moment Monk seemed at a loss for words, even for breath, and I was afraid of what he might say once he found both.

"I'm so glad that I was able to be here for it," Monk said.

"Me, too," Ambrose said.

"But there's a problem." Monk pointed at

Ambrose's legs. "You have a stain on your knee from kneeling on the wet grass."

Yuki stepped back so Ambrose could look at his knees.

"It's been so long since I've had stained pants," Ambrose said. "As I recall from Mother, grass stains are notoriously difficult to clean."

Monk nodded grimly. "I'm afraid they might never come out."

Ambrose dropped to his other knee and when he rose again, he had matching stains on both legs. It didn't surprise me that he did that. He was a Monk, after all, and symmetry is everything to them.

"I hope that's true, Adrian. I'm going to treasure these filthy pants." Ambrose seemed to notice Devlin for the first time. He extended his hand to her. "Pardon me, I don't believe we've met. I'm Ambrose Monk."

"Lieutenant Amy Devlin," she said. "Congratulations on your engagement."

"Thank you," he said. "I'll be serving marshmallows, Strawberry Pop-Tarts, and Fiji water in the house in a moment. But first, if you will all excuse me, I'd like to take a stroll around the block with my fiancée."

Ambrose offered his hand to Yuki. She

took it. And together they walked slowly, hand in hand, down the tree-lined street, Ambrose carefully avoiding the cracks in the sidewalk.

We watched them until they disappeared around the corner. Devlin shook her head.

"A Cap'n Crunch ring?" she said.

Monk took a pair of tweezers from his pocket and plucked a dog hair from Devlin's coat. "They are quite rare."

"They're plastic and come from a cereal box," she said.

"Anyone can buy a diamond." Monk examined the hair, then put it in a fresh baggie and sealed it. "He's been saving that ring for the right woman for nearly fifty years."

"So do you think she's the right woman, Mr. Monk?" I asked.

"The tattooed, ex-con biker chick who stole a million dollars and pushed a man in front of a bus?" he asked.

"Yes," I said. "Her."

Monk shook his head. "No, that's not her anymore. Now she's the woman who got my brother out of the house. That makes her the right one."

Monk, Devlin, Yuki, and I sat around the dining room table with a glass of Fiji water, an empty plate, and a knife and fork in front of each of us as Ambrose brought in a platter of Strawberry Pop-Tarts and a bowl of marshmallows.

"I've never been served Pop-Tarts and marshmallows together before," Devlin said.

"That's because only the most rare and special events merit such a combination of delights," Ambrose said, as he used tongs to place a Pop-Tart on her plate. "Be careful, it's hot."

"Two thousand years ago, marshmallows were a delicacy reserved only for the gods and the pharaohs," Yuki said, repeating a factoid that I know she learned from Ambrose. "It was a crime for anyone else to eat them. But now that anybody can have a marshmallow, we take them for granted. Serving them at moments like this reminds us to appreciate the little things that bring joy to our lives."

"And Pop-Tart, also known as a toaster pastry, is simply an ingenious confection," Ambrose said, standing at the head of the table and carefully handling his Pop-Tart with a cloth napkin. "It's a slice of pie in a convenient rectangular shape that eliminates the mess, requires no cutting, and guarantees consistent portions."

"It would be better if it was a square,"

Monk said, cutting his Pop-Tart with a knife and fork. "However, the Pop-Tart measures three inches by four inches, and that's twelve square inches, which is a good even number. The Pop-Tart itself is a model for concise, efficient, and conscientious meal preparation and delivery."

"Serving marshmallows and Pop-Tarts together is a culinary celebration that reflects the joy of whatever occasion you are recognizing," Ambrose added.

"I never gave much thought to marshmallows and Pop-Tarts," Devlin said. "I didn't know that anybody did."

"It's why pausing for reflection to acknowledge our joy is so important," Ambrose said, casting an adoring glance at Yuki. "And I am overflowing with joy right now."

"So why aren't you joining us at the table?" she asked.

"Because there're only five of us," Ambrose said.

"It's a big table," she said. "There's plenty of room."

Monk shook his head. "You really don't want five people at the table."

"Why not?" Devlin asked.

"It's uneven," I said.

"The table won't tip over," Devlin said.

"But the earth may slip ever so slightly off

337

its axis," Monk said. "It's a matter of cosmic balance."

"You're kidding me, right?" Devlin said.

"Sure, it seems small to us in this room," I said, "but if everybody was so cavalier about balance, and all at the same moment, the results could be catastrophic."

"You buy into this?" Devlin said to me.

"I've learned to adapt," I said.

"I've learned to love it," Yuki said, smiling at Ambrose.

"I feel like I'm dining with the Addams Family," Devlin said.

"Perhaps we should meet them sometime," Ambrose said. "I'm ready to widen my social circle."

Ambrose, it probably goes without saying, shared his brother's inability to detect sarcasm and lack of general knowledge regarding the keystones of American popular culture (the exception being *Beyond Earth*, Ambrose's favorite television program).

Devlin's cell phone rang. She answered it quickly, as if she was grateful for the interruption.

"Devlin," she said, then listened for a moment. "We're on our way." She hung up. "That was the captain. We're being summoned to the Federal Building."

"That's good," Monk said, setting his knife and fork down and pushing his plate away. "Because we still have a murderer out there to catch."

"Give me thirty seconds," Ambrose said. "I'll get you a Pop-Tart and marshmallows to take to the captain."

Ambrose hurried into the kitchen. Yuki discreetly got up and followed him, closing the door behind her.

"Do you know who the killer is?" I asked Monk, wondering if I'd missed his tell in all the excitement.

"Not yet, but I think we're close to a solution."

"We are?" As far as I knew, we had absolutely nothing to go on. "What have I missed?"

"Everything," he said.

CHAPTER TWENTY-EIGHT: MR. MONK FINDS BALANCE

We didn't get the Pop-Tart and marshmallows for the captain after all. Yuki made Ambrose forget all about them and we slipped quietly out of the house without saying good-bye.

I'm sure Ambrose and Yuki didn't mind.

Devlin drove us back into the city. I rode in the front beside her while Monk sat in the backseat, labeling the bags of dog hair from Jeroen Berge's house that he'd collected off of us throughout the day.

It was not uncommon to see him labeling bags of trash that he intended to throw out. He believed that even garbage should be organized.

We parked on the street in a red zone and went through the checkpoint in the lobby, where we were treated to an unusual amount of scrutiny as a result of our recent encounters with the security staff. The only thing they didn't do was give us a full cavity search.

When we were finally through the check-point, Special Agent Cardea was called down to escort the three of us directly to Thorpe's tiny office, where Stottlemeyer was already waiting in one of the four guest chairs. It was a tight fit.

The office had a window with a view, but the room itself was substantially smaller than the rolling, half-million-dollar crime lab and command center that Thorpe had occupied when he was on the fast track within the Bureau.

"I want to make sure that you two appreciate the severity of this situation," Thorpe said to Monk and me. "Your irresponsible rogue conduct put dozens of people in danger and led to the destruction of seven vehicles and one restaurant, and could quite possibly lead to criminal charges against you both."

Devlin gave me a thumbs-up behind Stottlemeyer's back.

"I'm in agreement with Thorpe," Stottlemeyer said. "I would never have condoned an operation like this, certainly not without much more planning, backup, and crowd control."

"That's why we didn't tell you about it," I said.

Devlin nodded approvingly. "I've definitely underestimated you."

"I don't appreciate it," Stottlemeyer said. "It's a miracle nobody was hurt or killed."

"If anybody was put at risk, it was Blackthorn that did it, not me," I said. "You seem to be forgetting that they kidnapped Yuki, disobeyed a direct order from a police officer to stand down, and drove backward down a one-way street."

"You should have anticipated that they might try to run," Stottlemeyer said.

"I did," I said. "That's why I called you."

"After your operation was already in play," Stottlemeyer said.

"Blackthorn and their operatives will get what's coming to them," Thorpe said to me. "And so will you."

"Natalie found your missing money and exposed a kidnapping plot," Monk said. "What she should get is full credit for the arrests and a commendation."

"She's not the only one in trouble here, Monk," Stottlemeyer said. "You are, too. With me. You figured out where the money was while you were at Jeroen Berge's house and you didn't tell me about it. I'm very disappointed in you."

"Who is Jeroen Berge?" Thorpe asked, scratching his hand.

"You've never heard of him?" Monk said.

"We wouldn't be asking if we had," Cardea said.

"You're aware that the mailman, Irwin Deeb, intercepted the stolen money that was sent to a mail drop and that he ran off with it," Monk said.

"We know," Thorpe said, leaning back in his chair and putting his feet up on his desk. "That's why we've got him in custody. Get to the point."

"When Michelle Keeling killed herself, Irwin thought she'd been murdered by whoever actually stole the money," Monk said. "So he went on the run, hiding out in homes that he knew would be empty because the owners had submitted vacation holds for their mail. One of those homes was Natalie's, another was Jeroen Berge's."

"Okay, so how did Berge end up dead?" Cardea asked.

"Because the inside man who actually stole the money from the evidence room figured out what Irwin did, and how Irwin was hiding, and went looking for him and the money in empty houses, including Berge's," Monk said. "But Berge came home early, walked in on the intruder, and got killed for it."

"And how do you know Irwin wasn't the

343

intruder who killed Berge?" Stottlemeyer asked.

"Berge died of a broken neck from a kick to the head by someone who is skilled in martial arts," I said. "That's definitely not Irwin."

"But it's the hair that definitively proves it wasn't him," Monk said.

"What hair?" Thorpe asked.

"Jeroen Berge owned a golden retriever that he foolishly allowed to lie on his recliner," Monk said. "Captain Stottle-meyer, Lieutenant Devlin, and Natalie all had to sit on it even though it was blanketed with dog hair."

"It was a Captain's Chair," I said in my defense.

"My God," Cardea said. "I envy you. Was it the one with the built-in Dolby Surround speakers?"

"It was," I said.

"Everyone who sat in the chair ended up covered in dog hair," Monk said.

"He's exaggerating," Devlin said. "It was a strand or two."

"I collected these samples from the three of them during the course of the day," Monk said and laid out three baggies, labeled with our names and the time the hairs were collected, on Thorpe's desk. "I also collected a sample from Yuki, who got some dog hair on her when she hugged Natalie outside the post office. Dog hair is like a disease — it spreads on contact."

Monk placed another baggie on the desk.

"I don't see what this proves," Cardea said.

"It proves why you shouldn't let animals on your furniture," Monk said.

"How is that relevant to what we are talking about?" Thorpe asked.

"It proves that you're having an illicit sex affair with Special Agent Nesbo," Monk said, "the woman who works in the evidence room."

Thorpe laughed. "You ought to try reading tea leaves instead of dog hairs because you're way off. I can do better than Nesbo."

"Perhaps you could," Monk said, "but you were using her to gain access to the evidence room and steal the marked money."

"Thorpe is the inside man?" Stottlemeyer said.

"And he killed Jeroen Berge," Monk said.

It was an astonishing accusation but, then again, most of Monk's usually are. And he's always right about this stuff, as I knew Thorpe would soon discover for himself.

I didn't know how Monk had proven it but it was going to feel especially sweet to see Thorpe go down.

Thorpe took his feet off the desk and stood up in outrage. "If you didn't know this man was insane before, this ought to make it abundantly clear."

"I'll agree it sounds crazy," Stottlemeyer said. "But it won't when he's done."

"It's really quite simple," Monk said to Thorpe. "Agent Nesbo owns a dog, a Jack Russell terrier and shih tzu mix. The dog sheds an enormous amount of black and white hair, some of which you picked up on your clothes in your intimate encounters with Nesbo. I pulled those same hairs off of Captain Stottlemeyer, Lieutenant Devlin, Natalie, and Yuki. That's how I know that you also sat in that chair. Because when you did, you left those hairs behind and picked up the golden retriever hairs that are on you now."

Thorpe immediately brushed himself, as if that would change anything.

"Okay, maybe I've been enjoying a little afternoon delight with Agent Nesbo. I admit that," Thorpe said. "But that's how I got this hair on me. It's from her. What you've proved is that she's the one who stole the money and killed Berge, not me."

"It makes sense," Devlin said.

"Not if you've ever met her," I said. "She

was shot in the knee in 2009. That's why she was reassigned to the evidence room. She couldn't possibly have delivered the fatal kick."

"But you are a martial artist," Monk said to Thorpe. "That's why you keep scratching your hands."

"It's because I have dry skin," Thorpe said.

"From taping your hands and wrists for martial arts bouts," Monk said. "Agent Nesbo might have been in on the theft with you, but you're the killer."

We were all staring at Thorpe now, who was beginning to perspire. He looked around the room.

"C'mon, this is craziness," he said. "Listen to what he's saying. His accusations are based on dog hair and dry skin, for God's sake. It's ridiculous. Yes, I'll admit I've been having some office nookie, but that's it. I didn't steal the money and I've never been in Berge's house."

"Not according to your desk," Monk said.

"What?" Thorpe said, practically yelling. "You're saying my desk was involved in the murder?"

"Berge's home is landscaped with distinctive gravel that easily gets stuck in the treads of shoes," Monk said. "This gravel right here."

Monk gestured to several tiny bits of stone, hardly bigger than grains of sand, on the desk blotter.

"Good God, Thorpe, it really was you," Cardea said.

Thorpe looked at the gravel and closed his eyes for a long moment, his shoulders slumped in defeat.

"You've been running the investigation on your own crime to throw everyone off the trail," Cardea continued. "You've made a clown out of me and the Bureau."

"You've always been a clown, George," Thorpe said.

I'd had enough of Thorpe and his arrogance. I stood up. "Does anybody have a set of cuffs?"

Devlin tossed me hers. I caught them and approached Thorpe. "Turn around and put your hands behind your back."

Thorpe looked over at Cardea. "You can't let her do this. If I am going down, it can't be by a lowly police officer from some piss-ant speck of a town. It's got to be a fed."

"Who, me?" Cardea said. "I'm a clown, remember? Besides, she deserves this after the misery we've put her through."

I put the cuffs on his wrists. "You're under arrest for the murder of Jeroen Berge and the theft of five hundred thousand dollars from the evidence room of the Federal Building."

"I can't believe this is happening to me," Thorpe said, shaking his head.

I read him his rights. It felt great and I noticed that Stottlemeyer was smiling, too. He didn't like Thorpe any more than I did. I was hoping this meant I wouldn't face any negative repercussions for my plan going ever so slightly awry at the post office.

"What were you thinking, Thorpe?" Devlin asked. "Why would you throw away your career for a lousy five hundred thousand dollars?"

"My career was already over. I was going nowhere in the Bureau," Thorpe said. "I messed up on just one case, the one Monk got involved in, and they took everything away from me — the high-profile investigations, my special unit, my mobile command center — and assigned me to this pitiful closet to handle the piddly crap. Me, a rising star, the best of the best. It was a waste of talent, of my God-given potential. So I decided to get out with a golden parachute."

"What was Nesbo's excuse?" I asked.

"She didn't know anything about it," Thorpe said. "I was screwing her in the office just to get behind the cage in the evidence room without having to log in."

"No pun intended," Devlin said.

"You had to know you were stealing marked money," Stottlemeyer said.

"Of course I did," Thorpe said. "I was going to launder it through accounts in the Cayman Islands. It would have worked, too, if I wasn't cursed."

"You mean incompetent," I said.

"My plan was perfect," Thorpe said. "What were the odds that the box would break, and that the mailman would run off with the cash, and that he'd hide out in the house where Monk's assistant lives? Bottom line: I've been cosmically screwed."

Monk shook his head. "No, it's just the natural balance of the universe."

"Let's go." Cardea gathered up the bags of hair and led Thorpe out of the room. When they were gone, the captain turned to Monk.

"You think his downfall was fate?" Stottlemeyer said. "I didn't know you believed in a higher power."

"I don't," he said. "I believe in balance. Don't you feel it?"

Stottlemeyer nodded. "As a matter of fact, Monk, I think I do."

I did, too.

I got all the credit for solving the case and it truly was the great going-away present that Monk had intended it to be.

The publicity I received for the arrests reached all the way to Summit, where Chief Disher and his police department really needed the positive press after the local government corruption scandal.

And it was good for me, too.

I would be returning to Summit to continue my new job as a police officer without having to worry about anyone questioning my qualifications to wear the badge.

More important, though, I wouldn't be questioning them myself anymore, either.

I didn't press any charges against Irwin Deeb, and neither did the other people whose homes he temporarily occupied, so he wasn't arrested. But the postal service fired him. They couldn't ignore what he'd done, though at least they didn't pursue criminal charges of their own.

He called and asked me out on a date, but I declined as politely as I could. I told him that I didn't want to begin a relationship now since I was about to move clear across the country to start a new job. It wouldn't be fair to him.

He took it well.

The stress of making all the arrangements for the move to Summit, the laborious task of packing up all of my belongings, and the sheer anxiety of getting my house rented distracted me from feeling the emotions of the change that I was making.

The emotional side wasn't so much the house anymore, or being separated by thousands of miles from my daughter, or the prospect of the challenges facing me in Summit.

It came down to just one thing.

Adrian Monk.

Working for him was the longest job that I'd ever held and it was also by far the most aggravating, frustrating, dangerous, exciting, challenging, and fulfilling one of my life. It was also one of the worst paid.

And on a strictly personal level, if you don't count my late husband, my relationship with Monk was the most enduring, and in some ways the most intimate and emotionally complex, that I'd ever had with a man.

Or anyone.

It wasn't over, either. It was just changing. Even so, I was going to feel his absence in my daily life more profoundly than anything else that I was leaving behind.

And I knew he'd feel it just as deeply, even though he was staying home and continuing, as best he could, with his life as it was before.

I couldn't leave him without making sure there was someone he could rely on until he found a new assistant. I knew he was more self-sufficient than he'd ever been before, and that the captain would be around. Still, he'd need someone to run interference for him, to drive him places, and to help him deal with the simple, everyday tasks in life that are accomplished easily and even mindlessly by you and me, but that can become insurmountable for him and drive him crazy.

Literally crazy.

The problem was, I had no idea where to find someone with the right temperament, who not only could handle his eccentricities and his demands but would be at ease taking him to a bloody crime scene.

Julie came over one night to help me pack

and to sort through all of her old stuff, so I shared my predicament with her and, to my astonishment, she volunteered for the job. At least temporarily.

She didn't do it as a favor to me or out of any great affection or concern for Monk. She did it because she needed money and couldn't find a more flexible part-time job that she could fit around her class schedule (though you can never predict when a murder might happen).

Monk was glad, and I'm sure more than a little relieved, to have her as a temporary assistant, although he framed it more as an opportunity for him to step in as a surrogate parent in my absence and to provide all the life lessons that I'd failed to impart.

"For instance, I'll introduce her to disinfectants and cleansers," he said, "and I'll instruct her in the proper use of a handy implement that we, in the civilized world, call a broom."

I didn't share any of that with Julie, of course. I didn't want her to quit before she even got started.

When my last day in the city finally came, I had Julie take me to Monk's apartment on our way to the airport so I could make sure the two of them were all set and so I could say good-bye.

We gathered in Monk's living room and I handed Julie my big purse.

"You're going to need this now," I said. "It holds a day's supply of Wet Ones, evidence bags, Fiji water, rubber gloves, and Advil."

She slung it over her shoulder and looked at Monk. "I didn't know that he took pain relievers."

"He doesn't," I said. "They're for you. So are the Rolaids."

"I make it look easy," Monk said, "but this is a stressful job."

She furrowed her brow. I'm sure she was wondering whether he genuinely didn't get what I was saying or if he was playing with her. She'd have to learn to figure that out on her own.

"Don't worry about Julie," Monk said. "I'll take good care of her while you're away."

"I think it's the other way around," Julie said. "I'll be taking care of you."

Monk shook his head. "Your mother thought the same thing when she started to work for me and look how it turned out."

He had a point. I felt myself getting choked up. I cleared my throat and willed myself not to cry.

"I'm going to miss you, Mr. Monk."

"I'd like it if you'd call me Adrian."

"I'll be back to visit and I'll probably call you a lot for advice."

"I'd like that," Monk said.

I took a step forward and gave him a hug, which he didn't resist, and I kissed him lightly on the cheek. As I pulled away, he kissed me back, taking me utterly by surprise.

I guess it showed on my face.

"I hope I didn't offend you," he said.

"No, of course not. It was sweet," I said. "It's just that you've never kissed me before."

"I couldn't. Up until now, you were my employee. But now you're my best friend."

I might have lost it, and started sobbing like a baby, if the doorbell hadn't rung at that precise moment.

"I'll get it," Julie said and went to the door.

She opened it and I was stunned to see Ellen Morse standing outside. But I wasn't half as stunned as Monk was. He froze.

"Hello, may I help you?" Julie said.

"My name is Ellen Morse," she said. "And you must be Julie Teeger."

"Have we met before?" Julie asked.

"No, but you have your mother's eyes," Morse said, smiling at me. "And her purse. May I come in?"

Julie looked back at Monk and me for approval, but we were both too surprised to say anything.

"Mr. Monk?" Julie prodded.

"Yes, of course, come in," Monk said, stepping forward to greet her. "What are you doing here?"

"You didn't leave me much choice," she said. "You told me you weren't coming back."

"I hope you didn't come here to try to talk me out of it because my mind is made up."

"No," she said. "I came here to be with you."

"For a visit," he said.

"For good," she said.

Monk rolled his shoulders and tipped his head from side to side as if he'd just solved a crime. He hadn't, of course. What he'd achieved was balance. A woman he loved was leaving his life and now another woman that he loved, even if he couldn't admit it to himself, was stepping in. It was the universe keeping things in order.

Experiencing balance like that was as close to happy as he ever got. I hoped Morse could sense that.

"But what about your home?" Monk asked. "And your store?"

"I can sell crap anywhere, Adrian," she said. "But I don't think I can be happy anymore without you. So I'm moving to San Francisco."

"You are?"

"I'm standing here, aren't I?" she said. "You haven't said that you're glad to see me."

"I am, of course," Monk said. "But the chances are that this isn't going to work out."

"We won't know until we try," she said.

"I just thought of something great," he said. "If you're moving here, you don't have to sell poop anymore. You can make a clean break. And I want to emphasize *clean*."

"She sells poop?" Julie said.

"All kinds," I said.

"I'm going to keep my store in Summit and open up another one here," Morse said.

"But you could get a respectable job instead," he said.

"And you could stop investigating murders and do something that isn't so bloody and grim," she said. "Like working with me."

"When hell freezes over," Monk said. "And you'll know when that happens because your store will be encased in ice."

Adrian Monk was staying home, and

keeping his old job, but I could see that he was in for some tumultuous changes, too, whether he liked it or not.

I was so happy I could have broken into song, but I suppressed the urge. I walked to the door with a smile on my face while Monk and Morse continued their argument.

"It looks like there are going to be some exciting times ahead for all of you," I whispered to Julie as I passed her.

"Easy for you to say," she said, joining me and closing the door behind us. "You won't be around."

I took my daughter's hand and gave it a squeeze. "But I can't wait to hear all about it."

ABOUT THE AUTHOR

Lee Goldberg has written episodes of the USA Network television series *Monk,* as well as many other programs. He is a two-time Edgar® Award nominee and the author of several other books, including *The Walk, Watch Me Die, The Dead Man,* and the acclaimed *Diagnosis Murder* novels, based on the TV series for which he was a writer and executive producer. His previous *Monk* novels are available in paperback, including *Mr. Monk and the Two Assistants,* which won the Scribe Award for Best Novel from the International Association of Media Tie-In Writers.

The employees of Thorndike Press hope you have enjoyed this Large Print book. All our Thorndike, Wheeler, and Kennebec Large Print titles are designed for easy reading, and all our books are made to last. Other Thorndike Press Large Print books are available at your library, through selected bookstores, or directly from us.

For information about titles, please call:
(800) 223-1244

or visit our Web site at:

http://gale.cengage.com/thorndike

To share your comments, please write:

Publisher
Thorndike Press
10 Water St., Suite 310
Waterville, ME 04901